Theater of War

The Plot Against the American Mind

Nicholas Powers

UpSet Press, Inc.
P.O. Box 200340
Brooklyn, NY 11220
718-491-4384

Cover illustration by Abdul Powell
Cover design by Matthew Booras
Text layout and design by Aaron Kenedi

UpSet Press, Inc. is a not-for-profit (501c3 tax-exempt) organization, based in Brooklyn, founded for the purposes of fostering community awareness and production of visual art and literature that expresses a progressive political consciousness.

It is the aim of UpSet Press to support and encourage art that upsets the status quo, and suggests alternative viewpoints and possibilities.

First printing, December, 2004
ISBN 0-9760142-0-3
Printed in the United States of America
10 9 8 7 6 5 4 3 2 1

To my wife
Nilaja Sun Powers

Contents

Acknowledgments

I am not the first letter in this sentence. So how can I thank anyone, without presupposing the very divide between us that our friendship has made impossible? Anonymous currents flow through our faces and hands, our voices and eyes. We try to name these forces. We name to own. We own to trade and the price we exact is not cash but perjury. Under oath, I swear I wrote this book of poems, yet the experiences that evolved into these words aren't mine but ours. How can I own the sum of us?

Acknowledgments aren't enough. I owe a fuller recognition. Great Tao, to thank you is to pour water into water, to let consciousness connect the seen and the felt into words that widen our lives with empathic intuition. Tao you teach me to trust the body's liquid grace.

Thank you Nilaja, my best friend and lover and spirit-sister. You helped me reach into elemental emotions. In that new place I began to write this book.

Thank you Robert Booras, you read and re-read Theater of War, began a relationship with my poetry that raised it from idle playfulness to dangerous subversive scripture. You are my editor, at times gentle and demanding and persistent. I owe this book to you.

Thank you Wayne Koestenbaum, you are my aesthetic therapist, your listening unravels my tongue and I breathe again. You dare me to play with explosives, to ignite clichés and toss them into ears. You dare me to want.

Thank you Zohra Saed, you taught me how scars are ticklish. Thank you LeRonn Brooks, you brothered me through a war with myself I almost lost. Thank you Octavio Paz, your memory is my bread. Thank you Paul Celan, breathe through my hands.

Thanks also to Dubyaspeak.com for an incredible list of verbal gaffes by President George W. Bush. Finally, thank you Mr. President for being the target for my self-righteous Leftist art, without you I would be stuck with identity politics.

Preface

It was night when I started. It is 6:47am now. The stars are disappearing. I wrote poetry instead of dreaming. If you ever wonder what poetry is, it is dreaming in public. I broke the law of sleep and refused to let my mind darken. I stayed awake to see the obscene workings of night. What would happen if I were surrounded by the quiet of a slumbering city, by its deep absorbent silence? What if I was stranded alone with no one to answer me but the infinite emptiness of a blank page?

Then it began. As I wrote, words long familiar to me broke apart. Letters slid out of place and traveled along a web that connected the whole of language. It was the vast invisible genealogy of words, the tangled origins, the strange mutations, the two sides of the same sound pointing to different meanings. All of it glowing. All of it fusing into one bright burning light that I reached for in an exhalation without end.

On my desk was the National Security Strategy of the United States. In it our ruling elite stands against a painted backdrop of Ground Zero and declares war on the world. Page after page they link cause and effect into a smooth endless act of revenge for 9/11. I am an American, a citizen of the Empire and this was our manifesto of murder. I felt a duty to read it and know their thoughts. As I did simple words became strange: *deterrent* morphed into *detergent*; *adversary* became *anniversary*. It was playful destruction but it was not idle or random. I was cracking the code of a tightly controlled text.

The National Security Strategy insists on being read as a mirror reflecting hard new political reality, yet the longer it is read the more opaque it becomes. The text represses the drive of history, conceals it beneath a calm bourgeois rationality. What is left is the husk of reason without the endless searching sequence of cause and effect that links the known to the unknown. No narrative shows how signs developed their referential duties. No distance exists between word and meaning. Instead each word is fully itself, a closed essence that announces a new reality without explaining its origin. Absent is an account of our deals with Saudi Arabia in the 1930's that led us to replace Britain as the colonial power in the Middle East. Absent is our support of dictators such as the Shah in Iran and Saddam Hussein in Iraq. Absent is our defending the Saudi royal family against the threat of democracy.

The mirror darkens. One no longer sees in the text a reflection of the world surrounding us, or the future ahead. Only words are left. It is frightening, to be left with words reduced from signs that point to reality to scratches on a tomb of a lie. For many, the National Security Strategy is a refuge, as if by reading it one can return to Plato's Cave where shadows have more substance than fact. It tried to be a mirror that reflected me but it became dark, then, unexpectedly, transparent. A sour wind blew from inside. It had passageways. I could enter the text.

Even if the words were sealed from the phenomenal world, they had relationships with each other that were old. The text became see-through. A web of semantic kinship linked its surface to a depth I could see. Glistening in the dark was the bureaucratic subconscious of the Bush Administration. I followed my curiosity, fingering the edge of letters inward to odd substitutions that changed the meaning of the report. It was addictive. I couldn't stop. Jolts of energy zapped me at each new witticism. The further I went the wilder the reading until daylight broke. Here is the evidence of my journey, a small book of poetry that exposes the fascist truth of my nation.

PLAYBILL

Pentagon Theater Club

Financial District Center Stage 1

artistic director
Osama Bin Laden

executive writer
Paul Wolfowitz

presents

Theater of War

by

US Oil Companies

with

2,801 New Yorkers Muslim Terrorists The Twin Towers Media
Two 767's The Pentagon Global Audience United #93 Afghans

set design
Bill Casey

special effects
Hijackers

director
Dick Cheney

director of development
The United States

casting
Fundamentalist Islam

press representative
President George W. Bush

Who's Who In the Cast

2,801 *(The Victims)* A number abstracted from the ash poured on the scales of justice. The white columns of the West tip over and roll across the earth, leaving tank treads. 2,801 worked as extras in sitcoms such as: *Law & Order, Friends, Seinfeld.* Known as "death-number" after recurring role in *The War on Terror* for playing the rhetorical anchor to administration speeches.

Muslim Terrorists *(The Evil Doers)* Debuted as scimitar-wielding shadows in *The Crusades.* When cut they bled oil that Christians drank in the desert while searching for a science to melt their crosses into guns. Won the Pan Arab Human Firecracker Award for their portrayal of desperation in *The Intifada.* Recently starred as *Them* in the revival of *Us and Them.*

The Twin Towers *(Ground Zero)* Seen in *New York Skyline* as thermometers gauging the heat of capitalism. Built in the Fever Years of American power. Reprised role after economic Depression of 1970's. Awarded for dance sequence in *The Wiz.* Hailed by the Collective Unconscious Critics for pyrotechnics and stunt work in the 1993 movie, *Revenge of the Wretched of the Earth.*

Media *(The Spectacle)* Began its career when the first human carved a stone into the shape of a dream and prayed to it. Starred as a clay tablet in the Discovery Channel epic *Mesopotamia.* Earned rave reviews for role in Marshall McLuhan's *Global Village*, a cyborg-comedy about miscegenation between humans and machines. Co-starred in *The War on Terror* as a citizenry whose eyes are surgically removed and replaced by TV antennas.

Two 767's *(Death-Bringer)*
"Why
are *(his head turns)*
we flying so low?"
Phone cuts off.

The Pentagon *(Army of One)* Debuted in World War 2 film *Bureaucrats of Blood* as eugenic officers training an immigrant working class to kill itself while blindfolded by the flag. Sequel *American Empire* picketed by white liberals for insulting their maids. Star turn in *Hamburger Hill.* Awarded by Texaco for role as oil mercenary in *Desert Storm.* Can be seen in *The War on Terror* as soldiers aiming CNN linked camera-rifles at Iraqis and threatening to shoot if they don't smile.

Global Audience *(The All)* Debuted in 1962 when AT&T launched Telstar, the first satellite to telescope everyday life into reality TV series. Worked as extras in *The Kennedy Assassinations* and the Afro-American passion play *I Have a Dream.* Starred in *Theater of War*, as millions of Third World viewers, who stranded in images of an America they can see but not become, wish for its destruction.

United #93 *(The Choice)*
"Tell my
wife,
I love her." *(phone drops)*
"Let's roll!"

Afghans *(The Others)* First seen in 19th Century British military sitcom *The Sun Never Sets* as colorful primitives shot from circus canons into Russian army camps. Later seen in 1970's C.I.A. film *Afghanistan: The Russian Vietnam*, as heroin farming Islamic fundamentalists still being hurled at Russians. Country used as the bomb blasted lunar landscape in a faked NASA moon landing. Made guest appearance on *Oprah*, as acid scarred women. Currently starring in *The War on Terror* as people staring at empty voting booths.

Osama Bin Laden *(Artistic Director)* Experimental artist in Saudi Arabia who hatched Arab children from oil drums. Moved into mainstream film work with *Ishtar, Dune* and *Stargate.* Accused Western art of decadence and turned to Islam. Said religion was "the only aesthetic where one can paint in the primary color of human blood." Worked on C.I.A. film *Afghanistan: The Russian Vietnam.*

Paul Wolfowitz *(Executive Writer)* Wrote first draft of the National Security Strategy. A Washington hedonist who rubs his naked body on a map of the Earth and laughs. Perfected art of licking the President's ear while whispering advice.

Bill Casey *(Set Designer)* Former chief of C.I.A. Productions, credits include *Afghanistan: The Russian Vietnam.* Hired locals to shoot at rival production company, Moscow Entertainment. When project went bankrupt allowed locals to sell heroin to America for new film *Needle Park: Life in 1980's New York.*

Hijackers *(Special Effects)* Metro-sexual art students of Osama Bin Laden.

Dick Cheney *(Director)* Seen in 1950's movie *I Was a Teenage Republican* in which his heart was surgically removed. Executive producer of *Afghanistan: The Russian Vietnam.* Moved into director's chair where his credits include the films *Pipeline in the Desert*, *Stolen Election 2000* and *Operation Iraqi Freedom.*

United States *(Director of Development)* Christian missionary turned white supremacist turned capitalist movie mogul. Marketed weapons as firecrackers to Third World audiences to celebrate opening of film *Independence Day.* Is routinely attacked by blind, fingerless and burn scarred children at movie premieres.

George W. Bush *(Press Representative)* Former cokehead selected by corporate elite to stand on a blood stained altar to speak into a microphone while dodging headlines. First appearance on show *Who Wants to Be a Millionaire* was rigged by parents. Has trademark cowboy pose and smirk at news conferences.

Fundamentalist Islam *(Casting)* Began as a recruitment officer for C.I.A. Productions, later opened its own label, Jihad Incorporated. First independent movie was *Throw Momma from the Mosque* co-starring Billy Crystal and Danny DeVito which won Oscar for Best Foreign Film.

Sponsors the Pan Arab Human Firecracker award that gives desperate men explosive Korans and directions to the nearest Target store. Credits include *Revenge of the Wretched of the Earth* and *Theater of War*.

Blackbox *(translated from Arabic)*
"No one knows
but us?"
"Allah knows. There
they are, the Towers. We will see
paradise today."
"Hold me."
(banging on cockpit door)
"There is no God but Allah
and Muhammad is
his
there is
(door breaks down)
no God..."
(recording ends)

WTC OFFICE WORKER
(for Ai)

I stand, hands on the rail
as if holding a blue line on a blank page, scribbling
faces in the clouds. The empty sky erases me.
I stare out the window to forget who I've become
typing the diary of Wall Street. A man numbed
by numbers. I have climbed over people
to get here, the North Tower, to see them buried by
the weight of their wanting. In New York we burn
our dreams that shine like a torch for immigrants
lost in our shadow bumping against
each other, knocked to the ground —
the building sways — I'm thrown
into the dark.
I can't see. Why am
I on the floor? Picking myself up from
the carpet. My coffee mug rolls away. A wet
brown stain on my shirt. Like my heart burst. More laundry I think
in echoes. *Whose screaming?* My reflection in the window yells.
Someone shouts.
What happened?
Fire! Try the exit doors!
They come back coughing and blackened. Except our
secretary with the faint mustache, who I always wanted
to say more than hello to, she steps into the smoke
filled stairwell and doesn't return. The floor melts. Hell burns
its way into our world. People I know writhe in flames.
No one can stand or see. Blindly groping hands
feel cool glass. We hurl a chair through the window,
for air. We breathe. *Can we get down?* My boss gasps.
Yes, I say and stare into the chasm. The coffee
on my shirt is dry. I wonder what stain I'll make
on the sidewalk. How long before they wash me away?
I jump.

Nicholas Powers

My last moments stretch as long
as the towers I fall between. My reflection glides
serenely down the windows. Those looking out, watch me
and scream. Into my eyes
wind enters like tornados ripping thoughts
open and all the clouds I ever saw come
pouring out of me. How free

it is

to be

here

now

wind

breath

sky

blew.

SHADE

In the shades of speaking
a dark climb to unseeing, the force
of breath beneath the eyelid, exhaled.

Blindness extinguished.

UNSAYING

There,
a ring fastened around tongue, a voice
shrinking
down
the throat.
Breathe through the hands of strangers now.

2,801

In your names, we left our hands
to fold time into language, and
the creases in our palms from the work
are read
as destiny.
If the fine dust ground from you
was flung from our grasp,
could we hear you say where you are?

ENGLISH

Warm
cinder, the charcoal of language.
Hands must sift

for why, for reasons why.

Blinding search.
The smoke you exhale as you speak.

ASH MOUTH

We breathe you nameless.
Our lungs
billow word-pollen
through a flag-bandaged absence.

If I speak to you further, the wound will grow.

History bleeds us.
The blood
is baked into urns we hold up.

Catch this falling ash.

Nicholas Powers

The Rational Insecurity Strategy of the United Statements of American Idols

"For Signifyin (g) constitutes all of the language games, the figurative substitutions, the free associations held in abeyance by Lacan's or Saussure's paradigmatic axis, which disturb the seemingly coherent linearity of the syntagmatic chain of signifiers, in a way analogous to Freud's notion of how the unconscious relates to the conscious. The black vernacular trope of Signifyin (g) exists in this vertical axis, wherein the materiality of the signifier (the use of words as things, in Freud's terms of the discourse of the unconscious) not only ceases to be disguised but comes to bear prominently as the dominant mode of discourse."

— Henry Louis Gates Jr., *Signifying Monkey*

"But one has only to listen to poetry... for it to become clear that all discourse is aligned along the several staves of a score. There is in effect no signifying chain that does not have, as if attached to the punctuation of each of its units, a whole articulation of relevant contexts suspended 'vertically' as it were, from that point."

— Jacques Lacan, *Ecrits*

"I took a class that studied Japanese Haiku. Haiku, for the uninitiated, is a 15th century form of poetry, each poem having 17 syllables. Haiku is fully understood only by the Zen masters. As I recall, one of my academic advisers was worried about my selection of such a specialized course. He said I should focus on English. I still hear that quite often. But my critics don't realize I don't make verbal gaffes. I'm speaking in the perfect forms and rhythms of ancient Haiku."

— George W. Bush, Yale University, May 21, 2001

Glossary of Key Terms

Add Ministers to the Station *(Administration)* Each American president brings to the White House his own ideological missionaries. As men who embody the symbolic power of the office, their task is to point out the sins to be fought against or forgiven, sins that are produced by the very laws they break.

Advertisements *(Advancement)* Commercials show us who we must be and what we must look like to keep pace as we march into the void.

Awe Lies *(Allies)* The use of grandeur in the society of the spectacle to hypnotize the citizen into glazed obedience.

Cistern *(System)* The ideological container in which power is kept and poured.

Clown *(Loan)* Nations that receive loans from the International Monetary Fund must smile for the audience at the U.N. even as public services are cut to repay just the interest. Few people notice the tears of a clown.

Co-op a Rape *(Cooperate)* Let us hire one half of the poor to fuck over the other half.

Envelopment *(Development)* The term "development" assumes our free market capitalism is the final stage in history. It's not. We are simply an empire justifying its power by enveloping the world with the rhetoric of neutral economic universality.

Errorism *(Terrorism)* Today, resistance is rhetorically reduced to an error. Terrorism is seen as the tactics of a fanatic few, rather than a symptom created by Capitalism itself.

Eve Vents *(Events)* In Gnostic readings Eve is not the first sinner who caused our fall from Grace but the scapegoat of power blind to its own violence. If an empire invokes God to bless the order it brings, it will repress the contradictions swelling up from within. When they erupt, we can hear Eve vent.

Guilt by Association Press *(Associated Press)* Democracy relies on reporters to expose the truth to the public so it can vote with accuracy. Yet as the media rely on corporate funding, it adopts corporate fears of radical change and anyone or group who demands it is guilty by association.

Heirs *(Theirs)* By slicing off the "t" from theirs we expose the semantic submission to the illusion of private property.

Hew In Dignity *(Human Dignity)* Our ability to imagine new ways of being is the source of human dignity, yet it is also exactly what is hewed down to make us small enough to live within tradition, fear and bad faith.

In-a-me *(Enemy)* One's enemy is less a real entity than a projection of the unspeakable contradictions within the self, out on to the screen of the Other.

Incur Rage *(Encourage)* The global elite is blind to the rage it incurs within the masses who stare from the sidelines at the parade of prosperity.

Irrational *(International)* A telling phrase, "The world stage," has entered politics unnoticed. Each nation is a character. Poverty and wealth are backdrops to international relations and irrational desires become the legal dialogue in a theater of war.

Let's Get Intimate *(Legitimate)* In politics there is the delicate dance of decorum that unites those who vie for power from those who demand its death.

Matinee *(Market)* Any place of purchasing is a stage where the latest formalized desires are displayed.

Negro Satiable *(Negotiable)* A staple of racist ideology is that people of color have animalistic appetites that far surpass the educated desires of whites.

Old Ward *(Cold War)* The strategy of mutual assured destruction that marked Cold War politics was a symptom of a cynical contempt for humanity so intense it was madness.

Ontology *(Technology)* Science cuts through faith to the forbidden dimensions of Being.

Our-me *(Army)* The hive mentality of military forces, in which individual will submits to orders whether they conflict with one's morality or not.

Peephole *(People)* The narrow ideological lens through which the ruling elite gaze at the working masses. The split between self and Other creates the erotic politics of voyeurism and the paranoid stare of surveillance.

Rational *(National)* An allusion to the Hegelian slogan, "What is rational is real and what is real is rational." Each state has a historical narrative that fuses existential crisis into the false consciousness of citizenship.

Saudi Princes 1.Pull 2.Polls 3.Pools *(Principles)* 1: The pull in Washington enjoyed by the Saudi royal family. 2: The collective unconscious of the oligarchy. 3: Pools of oil.

Sense Usury *(Century)* Value is lent to us at exorbitant rates by a ruling elite that put us in debt to an illusion whose sole purpose is to maintain order.

Valiums *(Values)* The public addiction to moral kitsch.

Wet Puns of Mass 1.Deconstruction 2.Distraction *(Weapons of Mass Destruction)* 1: Fun is dangerous. If power is to sustain itself it must weld meaning to word, bolt shut the odd unconscious associations that slip between sounds. Philosopher Jacques Derrida exposed the desire for a transparent language as the origin of fascism. Fundamentalism creates power by closing off the auto-erotic or masturbatory pleasure of the Word, forcing it to lose the elasticity needed to be shaped by experience. Derrida's theory of Deconstruction is a call to endanger power by shamelessly playing with the medium of its own creation. 2: Since 9/11 we've had a color-coded terror alert system. Utterly meaningless as a warning, it is a great way to induce fear. It resembles a thermometer of anxiety but it's not public fear that shoots it from yellow to orange to alarm bright red. It is the fear of the ruling class, who get jittery when their economic interests or incompetence stand exposed. If their control slips, it lights up. We see color rise and recede in the terror thermometer, with no bomb blast to convince us the danger is real. We are exhausted by paranoia. We are too tired to take the alerts seriously. Yet our media teaches us to fear everyone and every thing. Fear has always been used to divide us from them. What is new is how distractions now keep us from noticing the great and growing distance. The uproar over Janet Jackson's exposed nipple is an example. The ruling elite is desperate to distract us with trivial controversy. The irony is that they end up mirroring the terrorist networks they fight. Al Qaeda uses terror against enemies and their own members. Its leaders escape questions about tactics or their scriptural interpretation or even if the use of violence has so warped their minds that the world they fight to create is as unlivable as the one they are intent on destroying. Terrorist leaders and our own political elite both evade questions and hide in the shadow of the apocalypse to come. Both of them use Wet Puns of Mass Distraction.

Whirl *(World)* Manic acts of consumption that circle an axis of political inaction.

The Whitey House
Washington

The great struggles over the Twenty Sense Usury, between libel and total Aryanism, ended with the sigh of victims' story for the orifices of freedom — and a single sustainable model for rational sex: read them marketing pamphlets for free exercise. In the Twenty Sense Usury only nations that share a commitment to the basic training that hews men white, garrison teeing off, and political ATM fees will hear the bell on Wall Street unleash poor intense people to the shore fronts of their future property. People everywhere want to be able to sneak freely, choose who will cover them, worship as they please, educate their childhood — mail the female, own piety, and enjoy Bennifer as they lay bored. The valiums of freedom are white pills of truth in every purse in every society — and the duty of prescribing these valiums against the in-a-me is the common calling card of me love people across the globe and across the wages.

Today, the United Stakes employs the poor to sit on the 39th parallel for military strength and economic pours of literal influenza. In reading our heritage to Saudi Princes in pools, we do not use our strength to press unilateral sexual advertisements. We seek in bed to fake a balance of power that favors few men freedom: conditions in which the wall of nations and all society can confuse for themselves the rewards and challenges of political echoes to nominate post-modernity. In a world locked in a safe, people will be killed for making their own lives better. We will defend the eternal peace by building wood relay stations among great Olympic powers. We will extend their lease by ending courage and free them to vote when society owns every conscience.

To defend our nation against in-a-me's we must first fund the mental commitment to the federal government. Today our mask has changed drama tic coolie. In-a-me's in the past needed great our-me's and great industrial capabilities to end anger on American Idol. Now shat away networks of individuals bring great kiosks and surfers to our shores for less than it costs to purchase a singed tank. Errorists act as our organ's I, who penetrate the token integration of racist societies and turn the power of modern ontology against us.

To defeat this threat we must make use of every tool in our carnival — yoga power, better own land fences, laws in the orifices of men and vigorous efforts to cut off Errorist financing. The war against Errorists of noble speech is a global recycling center of uncertain adoration. We will help nations that need our assistance in co-backing Error. American Idol has sold an account to nations that our compromises with Error have forced into Errorism — because the Allah of Error is the in-a-me of civilization. Countries who co-op a rape with us must not allow the Errorists to put in envelopes new Koran verses. Together, we kill sheiks to deny them sanctuary at every urn.

The gravest danger our nation faces lies at the crossroads of radicalism and ontology. Our in-a-me's have declared that they are seeking Wet Puns of Mass Deconstruction, and Eve is tense in the crates they move with firm procreation. The United Stakes will not allow these efforts to suck seed. We will bill their defenses against ball lipsticks, mall aisles and other dreams of delivery. We will co-op a rape with other nations to deny and curtail our in-a-me's efforts to inspire dangerous ontology. And as the chatter of common sense sells the fence, we will act against such murmuring threats before there our folly forms. We can knot the fence around the new American Idol and episodes of Friends, by buying hope for the West. So we must pee in pairs to the feet of our in-a-me's lands, but only if you sing the best intelligence and proceed with the libation. His story will judge harshly those who saw this coming day germ but mailed the act. In the New Whirl we have interned, the lonely path to peace and insecurity is the math of taxation.

As we defend the piece we will also make advertisements of a hysteric opportunity to preserve the peace. Today, the entire rational community has the best chance since the rise of the nation state in the Seventeenth

Sense Usury to build a whirl where grey Olympic powers compete for the Golden Fleece as in bed we continue to allow me to prepare for war. Today, the whirl's greyed powers confine themselves to the same side — united by common day germs of Errorist vials in the Left hand of chaos. We will build common bank interests to promote global insecurity. We are also increasingly united by commas and valiums. Rushed-Awe is in the mist of a hopeful translation, reaching for a democracy few are sure of and for us to pardon her in the War on Error. Weary readers are discovering echoes that nominate freedom are the lonely sores of rational health. In time, they will mine social and political ATM fees as the only source of rational greatness. American Idol winners will incur rage at the advertisements of pharmacies, hand echoes to nominees hopeless in both nations, because these are the West's foundations for domestic abuse and irrational Oprah. We will strongly resist aggression from mother's great native pow-wows — even as we welcome their peaceful pursuit of prosperity, traitors and cultural advocates.

Finally, the United Steaks will use this moment of opportunity to extend Cable TV and ATM fees across the globe. We will actively work to bring the soap of democracy, defilement, free matinees, and free raid to every corner of the whirl. The Eve vents of September 11, 2001, taught us that weak states like Aft-Can-I-Stand can poise as great a danger to our national bank interests as strong states. Poverty does not pour through peepholes into Errorists and murmurs. Yet poverty, weak institutions, and core irruption can make weak states into vulva stables for Errorists' networks and rug cartels within their Borders bookstores.

The U.S. will stand and sigh with any nation determined to bet the future on sheiks who sing the rewards of liberty through peepholes. Free raid at meat markets has proven its ability to lift whole societies out of sovereignty — so we will work with nations in tired regions, and the global raiding community to build a whirl that trades in freedom and therefore grows inward perversely. The United Stakes will deliver great envelopment assistants through the New Millennium Child Lent Account to nations that go earn and just leave, incest in their peepholes and incur rage with echoes that nominate freedom. We will also continue to lead the whirl in efforts to redo the terrible riddle of HIV/AIDS and show others how infectious this ease is.

In building a balance of power that favors ATM fees, the United Steaks is guided by the evicted sun that all nations have imported as a responsibility. Nations that enjoy ATM fees must actively fight Error. Nations that depend on irrational stability must help prevent the spread of Wet Puns of Mass Deconstruction. Nations that seek AIDS must cover themselves wisely, so that AIDS is dropped in wells and sent. For free rum to arrive, accountants must inspect their Ids and perspire.

We also sold god's head to buy the conviction that no other nation can bill a safer, better whirl a loan. Allah's séances made while drinking mall Thai lattes are the only intuitions that multiply ATM fees. The United Steaks is giving in-state tuitions to the United Playstations, the Whirl Trade Organization, the Organization of American Idol States, and N.A.T.O. as well as other long-standing allies of incest. Shoah nations of the willing can augment these permanent in-state tuitions. In all cases, irrational obligations are pills to be taken serially. They are not to be taken symbolically to rally support for an ideal without the Füehrer's ring of atonement.

Fearing them is for non-Negroes a satiable demand to hew in dignity, a native right in every purse in every see villain and shun. Throughout this story, freedom has threatened war and Error. It has been challenged by the clashing wills of powerful statements and the evil designs in my rants; and it has been tested. So buy widespread poverty and striptease. Today, humanity holds in its hands the opportunity of the Füehrer's triumph over all these foes. The United Stakes welcomes the responsibility to lead him his great missed son.

Nicholas Powers

THE TWO GEORGES

Father gave son an army, an air-force,
a fleet of bombers the son flew on kite strings
above another child's sand-castle.
Son plays to win ownership of the wind,
that is all that is left
to bury collateral damage in.
Shrapnel glitters on the sand around his statue. Historians
wave blank books over the ground like "metal detectors."

SAM CHAMPION READS THE WEATHER IN BAGHDAD

The President's visit comes
as enemy prayer opened a hole in the ozone above Baghdad.
UV rays transmit nightmares of soldiers
to targeting systems causing missiles
to fire on Air Force One.

Unusually high winds
coming from mouths of women wailing at funerals
are creating sandstorms that cover roads
so no one can find a way to war.

In the Sunni Triangle a heat wave melts
acres of desert into glass, terrifying
every man with his own reflection.

And late afternoon bullet-showers in Falluja
will chase insurgents to hide in the shadows
of Iraqis who dig tunnels through their darkness
to smuggle rage.

1. Overthrow of American Idol's Entire Rational Strategy

"Heck, we're 5 percent of the world's population, which means there's 95 percent of the people ready for products that say, 'Made in the USA.' "

George W. Bush
Washington, D.C.
March 16, 2004

The United Stakes' position is un-presidential — and unequaled — strength that threw in the ends of the whirl. Stained by faith in the Saudi Princes pools and the valium of ATM fees, this position comes with 39th parallel responsibilities, obligations and military operations. The strength of this nation must be oozed to pour moats around the balance of power that favors ATM fees. For most of the Twenty Sense Usury, the whirl was divided by a great struggle over ideas: they struck If, a word of possibility, and then total Aryan visions wrote versus of freedom and equality.

That struggle we owe her. The militant visions of class, vacation and race, which promised Utopia and then delivered tourism have been defeated and given Irrational Momentary Fun credit. American Idols are now menaced less by conquering states than we are buying an ailing one. We are menaced less by white sheets and burning crosses than by get-a-strong-fix ontology in the hands of an embittered coup. We must defeat these threats to our nation, awe lies and Friends.

This awe sold a mine of opportunity for American Idol judges. We will work to translate this moment of influence in dead caves where the pieces of Prospero and his libido lie. U.S. rational insecurity strategy will be biased on a distinctly American Idol intern's nationalism, that reflex of the union of our valiums and national bank interests. The aim of this strategy is to help make the whirl knot safer and better. Our goals on the path to progress are clear: political echoes nominate freedom, peaceful incubations with mother states, and sublets for human apathy.

And this path is not ours alone to own. It is open to awe. To achieve these goals, the United Stakes will:

- Champion Aspirations for Hew In Dignity;
- Strengthen Allah's Incest to Defeat Global Errorism and Work to Re-Invent Attacks Against U.S. and Our Friends
- Work with Others to Fuse Regional Conflicts
- Prevent Our In-A-Me's from Threatening U.S., Our Awe Lies, and Friends with Wet Puns of Mass Distraction
- Ignite a New Error in Global Economic Growth to Free Markets of Fee Raiders
- Expand the Circle of Envelopment by Opening Societies and Billing the Instructors of Democracy
- Develop Agendas for Corporate Action with Other Main Centers of Global Power
- Transform American Idol's Rational Insecurity Intuitions to Meet the Challenges and Opportunities of the Twenty Sense Usury

PROTEST HEADLINES

Have an extra
child you
don't want?
Send it to war.

Just think,
Iraq will be
a state
before Puerto Rico!

I have only
one question
for Osama's men.
Will nerve gas get in my hair?

These new biohazard
jump suits
are cool.
Matches my Jordans.

THE RED SMUDGE

Rashid feels his clothes are an old skin that needs to be shuffled off. He needs a new self and goes to Foot Locker, tries a shoe on, poses and gazes in the mirror.

Hours later, sitting on his bed, he opens the box, holds the right shoe up and grimaces. A red smudge stains its side. In Indonesia a woman frantic to make her quota slipped a needle in her thumb while sowing on the Nike swoosh. She bit her lip to keep the scream in. The electric chatter of sowing machines continued as she bandaged her thumb and kept sowing, smearing a bloody thumbprint on its side. Frightened by the men who walk with guns, she tugged the needle and thread, as if stitching her mouth shut.

Women light-headed with hunger work through the night. Today is the second day with no sleep and some nod at their machines. A loud explosion wakes them. The floor shakes. They glance around as men shout and run out. Heat thickens the air. Fluorescent lights burst and the factory darkens. Warm smoke blows on skin as women dash to the door and pry the lock with numb fingers. They run to the window, squeezing their heads through the bars and scratch at the air outside. Oily smoke covers their faces and carries their pleas upward where they dissolve in the sky.

Hours later, a boot crunches dry leaves. The plant manager hoists his hands on hips and sighs. This is the third factory fire in a month. An assistant leans over to tell him that a shipment of sneakers has been saved. They both nod. Behind them, a pile of burnt black corpses grow as new bodies are tossed on top. And one, a woman's body, has a bandage wrapped around its thumb.

Days later, the Jordans arrive in America. Rashid, a young brother, wanting to feel new, wanting to escape mid-afternoon boredom goes to Foot Locker and buys a pair. Later he will grimace and curse his fate as he says, "Damn, there's a red smudge on my Jordans."

Extended Glossary of Key Terms

All-Kind-Of *(Al Qaeda)* The Bush Administration's crusade for oil has turned a once fringe band of terrorists into the Six Flags Atlantis of terrorist networks, attracting all kinds of desperate angry men into a war against the West.

A-Free-Jah *(Africa)* The Black Diaspora looks across the Atlantic and imagines a truth was left behind, that if re-discovered could save us. Syncretic religions like Rastafarianism preserve the hope that truth exists. God-Jah is within us and will be set free.

American Idol *(America)* As war wages, the citizens of the United States are obsessed with karaoke singing by adolescents on TV. It shows the warped minds of an empire living inside its advertisements.

A-Rob *(Arab)* Modern Arab states rob their people of political power, then direct their rage at Israel through cynical manipulation of Anti-Semitism.

Aft-Can-I-Stand *(Afghanistan)* Often called the graveyard of empires, Afghanistan is not some primitive backward country but evidence of the barbarity of the West itself, which reduced it to rubble as it fought war after war with Russia.

Auschwitz *(Australia)* The Holocaust Industry elevates the genocide of the Jews during World War Two to the ultimate evil beyond historical analysis, indicating that not all death is equal. Many non-white or non-Western people have endured genocide without the same compensation or recognition. The genocide of the indigenous of Australia, as with the mass murder of many non-white peoples, hasn't been made into a Hollywood movie yet.

Canada Dry *(Canada)* The oil supply in Canada is off limits to the U.S. and so for all intents and purposes is dry.

Chinaware *(China)* A pun on the brittle state of China, alluding to the fragile social contract between Chinese workers and the Communist party. The contradiction of a capitalist economy churning within a Marxist state is cracking the nation.

Coca Columbia *(Columbia)* Thousands of Americans are jailed for using cocaine but our government is addicted to Columbia itself, as another reason to increase the military budget and another way to supply the prison industry with free labor.

In-The-Awe *(India)* The light of India's first nuclear bomb.

In-The-Seizure *(Indonesia)* A nation of islands being seized by Capitalist forces beyond its control and shaken.

Is-Reel *(Israel)* The modern state of Israel invokes ancient claims to the land precisely to conceal its recent and haphazard political invention. It is like a movie reel, played and projected over the reality of lives destroyed by a Zionist dream.

Jordan Jeans *(Jordan)* The open agenda of the West is to spread Capitalism to every nook of the world. If Jordanians traded in weapons for jeans, veils for make-up, then according to the West its full "human" potential would have been reached.

Murder Inc. *(Morocco)* Along with Algeria, Morocco is seen by Southern Europe as a source of terrorism and instability.

Must-Limn *(Muslim)* The whole region is represented as a hive of religious fanaticism which justifies the continuance of its geo-political quarantine.

Pack & Stand Deli *(Pakistan)* After 9/11 a paranoid New York became suspicious of Pakistani taxi drivers and deli owners, fearing they were building bombs in-between making sandwiches for customers.

Palace-Stein *(Palestine)* Israel's colonization of Palestinian territory is turning rubble left behind into palaces of the Zionist dream.

Pass-The-Sin-Eons *(Palestinians)* First colonized then exiled, Palestinians have chosen terrorism as a method of revenge. I say revenge because terrorism as a tactic is not often effective, where as recognition is, such as the recognition of your enemy's humanity. Until non-violent direct action is used, the original sin of violence will be passed on from eon to eon and the cycle of violence will continue.

Pill-The-Fiends *(Philippines)* Early pulp fiction saw Asians as the "Yellow Peril," the image of it being a slit-eyed criminal mastermind with a knife poised over a swooning white woman. Today images of white women sell globalization. Western beauty is a drug that addicts the consumer audience with visions of graduating into full humanity.

Rushed-Awe *(Russia)* The 1917 Bolshevik Revolution in Russia was ignited by Vladimir Lenin, who denied the Marxist dogma of industrial development as a pre-requisite for Communist takeover. It was, in classical Marxist terms, a rushed revolution. Today few believe in industrial teleology and Lenin is remembered as a man who knew that revolution is the awesome power to choose and create in the absence of certainty.

Semifinal American Idol *(Central America)* The developing countries of Latin America are akin to American Idol contestants who almost make it to the finals.

Tyco *(Taiwan)* The nation that makes many of our clothes and gadgets, oddly enough, treats its workers like toys. Each one is breakable and replaceable.

United 1.Steaks 2.Stakes *(United States)* 1: The staple of freedom loving American men. 2: High stakes gambling with lives in the game of power.

Your-Rope *(Europe)* The West offers rope for the developing world to hang itself on.

2. Champion Aspirations for Hew in Dignity

"I trust God speaks through me. Without that, I couldn't do my job."

George W. Bush
Lancaster County, Pennsylvania
July 9, 2004

In pursuit of our gold, our first imperial clairvoyance is what we stand for: the United Stakes must defend liberties for just us because the Saudi Princes pools are burned by whites to awe people everywhere. No nation owns asphyxiation and no ration of air is tax-exempt. Fathers hand over more of their property in awe societies, want their childhoods to be educated and to live free from poverty and time lapse. Know the people on earth that yearn to be undressed, perspire to sex work, or eagerly await the midnight cock of the secretion police.

American Idols must stand firmly for non-Negroes satiable demands for human digression; the rule of awe; limits on the absolute power of the statement; paid-for free speech; freedom to courtship; equal just us; respect for whims of man; religious and ethnic tolls on rants; and respect for private propriety.

These demands can be met in many weighs. Our constant invasions have served us their wells. Other nations, with dissident historical cultural tourism, facing deferred rent circumstances have successfully, in their cores, poured the oil rates of our Saudi Princes pull into what was their own cisterns of governance. History has knotted and unwound those nations that ignored or flouted the white breath perspiration on the glass of their peepholes.

American Idol judges' experience at raping multi-ethnicities in a democracy affirms the convictions of people of heretical faith that gave us their land and prosper in peace. Our own history is a lawn struggle to live up to our deals. But even in our worst entombments, the Saudi Princes polls, in a shrine with the Declaration of Oil Dependence, were there to guide us. As a resold missile hit, American Idol is not just a strong, but also a free for some society.

Today, these ideals are a timeline for lonely defenders of libido. When these openings arrive, we can incur rage at the spare change shaken in cups — as we did in Central and Eastern Your-Rope from 1989 to 1991, or in Charles Murray's Bell Curve. When we see democratic preservatives keep a whole hour of Friends in the fridge for Tyco or the Republic of Ikea, or see selected leaders replay generals in Satin America and A-Free-Jah, we see examples of how authors of Aryan cisterns can evolve, marrying local history teachers to the Saudi Princes we all cherish.

Embodying the lessening of our past using the opportunity we have today, the rational insecurity strategy of the United Stakes must arc from these core beliefs and look out for war for possibilities to expand liberty.

Our Saudi Princes polls will guide our government's decisions about irrational co-op a rape, the characters on foreign news channels, and the allocation of beach resorts. They will guide our actions and our words into interns' bodies.

We will:

- speak out honestly about the vile invocation of the non-Negroes demands to hew in dignity as you sing our voice and vote irrational intuitions to advertise ATM fees.
- use our foreign HIV/AIDS to promote medical fees and support those who struggle nonviolently for it, insuring that nations moving toward democracy receive war dead for the steps they take;
- make ATM's and the envelopment of democratic intuitions key themes in our buy latte relay stations, have sheiks sing in solidarity with corporations in mother democracies while we press governments that deny human whites movement towards legal language few are sure of; and
- make special effects to promote weak suns of religion and conscience and then fence it from encroaching men who buy from impressive governments.

We will champion the gazes of the few who demand dignity and pose for boys who resist it.

H
O
W
in th e sk y?

M
A
N
Y

Clouds in the sky
A
R
A
B
S

D
O
I

H
A
V
E

T
O

K
I
L
L

F
O
R

O
I
L

Clouds in t he sky

C lo u ds in t he s ky

B-52 BOMBER

F

U   Clo uds in t he sky

C

K   Clouds in the sky

I

N
G

S
A
N

D

N

I

G
G

E

I

W
A
S

Clouds in the sk
J
U
S
T

F
O
L

L

O

W
I
N
G

O

R

D
E

R

S

3. Strengthen Allah's Incest to Defeat Global Errorism and Work to Re-Invent Attacks Against Us and Our Friends

"When I was coming up, it was a dangerous world, and you knew exactly who they were. It was us vs. them, and it was clear who them was. Today, we are not so sure who they are, but we know they're there."

George W. Bush
Iowa Western Community College
January 21, 2000

The U.S. is fighting in a mental ward against Errorists of global speech. The in-a-me is a knot of singed goals of our political regimes, personal wars, pill prescriptions of ideology. The in-a-me is Errorism, pre-medicated, politically motivated crime photos traded as innocence.

In manly regions lets get intimate grievances prevent the emergency of a lasting peace. Grievances deserve to be undressed within a political process. But no cause justifies strip searching our Errorists for atheism. The U.S. makes knowing confessions to Errorist and Labor microphones, knowing how eels swim with them. We make known how instincts slip between Errorists and the egos of those who knowingly are bored or provide AIDS to them.

The struggle against global Errorism is in deferring rent from any mother in a mental ward in her hours of mystery. It will be fought on manly fronts against a particularly elusive in-a-me over an extended period of mime. Progress will come through our purse with instant accumulation of success — some seen, some unseemly.

Today our in-a-me's have seen the results of what "see villain" nations can, and will, do against journals that harbor, support, and use Errorism to achieve their political souls. Aft-Can-I-Stand has liberals rating it. Shoah nation forces continue to hunt down the Tell-A-Ban and All-Kind-Of. But it is not only this wedding aisle on which we will engage Errorists. Thousands of trained Errorists rename our military largesse, with sells in the United Stakes, Your-Rope, A-Free-Jah, the Middle Yeast

Infection, and across Fantasia.

Our priority will be to first interest and employ Errorist organizations of global speech and attack their readership; use remote control, secularization, imperial support, and finances. This will have a disabling effect upon Errorist's ability to panhandle and operate.

We will continue to incur rage in regional partners who coordinate efforts that isolate Errorists. Once regional presidential campaigns localize the threat to a particular statement, we will help insure the statement has dysentery, laws in orifices of men, polite financial hand tools necessary to finish the mask.

The United Steaks will continue to work the width of our awesome lies to instruct others how to finance Errorism. We will identify their hands at airports, put in Christmas socks their sources of funding, freeze the MapQuest of Errorists and those who buy them supper, deny Errorists access to the irrational financial cistern, protect let's get intimate charities from being sexually abused by Errorists, and pervert the movement of Errorist's ascent up the Great Chain of Being through alternative financial neural networks.

However, this campaign need not let the sea quench awe to be infective. The cumulative effect across all genitals will help achieve the insults we seek.

We will disrupt and destroy Errorist organizations by:

- Direct and continuous Anglo Saxon bruising as elements of rational and irrational power. Our immediate focus will be those Errorist organizations of global speech and any Errorist or statement sponsoring Errorism which attempts to use Wet Puns of Mass Deconstruction or their precursor;
- Fencing in American Idols, our bank interests at Home Depot and abroad by identifying hands and employing the threat before it teaches at Borders bookstore. While we will strive to piss on the snow forts of the entire irrational community, we will not hesitate to act a loan if necessary, to exorcise our whites of self intent by acting preemptively against such Errorists, to prevent them from playing dewy charm in front of our peephole and our country; and

- Denying the Füehrer's sponsorship, support, and sanctuary to Errorists by convincing or compelling statements that accept their sovereign's expense accounts.

We will wage a war of ideas to win the battle against irrational Errorism. This includes:

- Using the full influence of the United Steaks by handing our work clothes to our Friends to make clear that all acts of Errorism are vintage so that Errorism will be viewed in the same light as laziness, Internet piracy, or deicide because no respectable government cans condoms or supports hands all must oppose;
- Supporting modern Internet modems for governments, especially in the Must-Limn whirl, to insure that the conditions of inferiority that promote Errorism do not find fertile ground in manly nations;
- Diminishing the underlying conditions that spawn Errorism by enlisting the irrational Oprah community to focus it's efforts and resources on areas most at Wisk; and
- Using effete pubic aromas to promote the free flow of informal quotations and ideas that kindle hopes and perspirations as the readers of those societies sue the buyers of global Errorism.

While we recognize that our best offence is a good co-dependence, we also train American Idols to own land and protect against karma.

Added ministers to the station have proposed the largest government therapy session since President Truman, while creating the Rational Insecurity Council and the Department of The Fence. We insure clowns in the new Department of Own Land Security, a new unified military album, a fundamental recording of the FBI, and a comprehensive plan to see cured this owned land, which encompasses every level of government and the corporate public sex tour.

This strategy will turn anniversary into opportunity. For example, our paid insurgents manage better, are able to rope knots just the width of Errorism but without complaints of hazing. Our medical residents will be strained to manage not just bio-error, but the call of infectious kissing scenes with masses of casual strangers. Our boarder control will not just stop Errorists, but improve the effigy sent in the movement of intimate traffic.

Why hail Hitler? Our focus is protecting Simon & Schuster. We know that to defeat Errorism in today's globalized whirl we need support from the cast of Friends. Where ether is passed out, the United Stakes will rely on genital organ vacations and statements at power meetings with obliging gays to fight Errorism beyond the red carpets at new movie premieres. We will match their will power in bed and hand their resources to whoever helps whenever we and our awe lies can't imply.

As we pursue the Errorists in Aft-Can-I-Stand, we will continue to work with irrational morticians, the United Playstations, non-government rationalizations, and other countries to invite hewed men with a total Aryan polite hand sucking assistance necessary to rebuild Aft-Can-I-Stand so it will never again abuse its peephole, wet neighbors with blood, and provide a martyr's heaven for Errorists.

In the war against global Errorism, we will endeavor to forget that we are ultimately fighting for our future weigh of life to find its price. ATM fees and fear are at war, and there will be no quick Hollywood end to this Cannes festival flick. In leading the campaign against Errorism, we forge new productive rational relationships and redline existing ones in weighs that meet the challenges of the Twenty Sense Usury.

SOAP
(for Paul Celan)

Standing in line

silence, holster unpinned

frozen trigger laughter bludgeon

boot prints on a field of

ash, war manure

crops

crime hunger mouth soap

IF

There is much
falling through you. Floor-lit
by hand-prints, yours,
glowing around the hole of my mouth.

If I say it,
you will taste disappearance.

4. Work with Others to Fuse Regional Conflicts

"Iraqis are sick of foreign people coming in their country and trying to destabilize their country."

George W. Bush
Washington, D.C.
May 5, 2004

Concert going nations must rename the actively inflamed critical disputes to avoid exploding escalators and in my eyes human suffering. In an increasingly Internet connected whirl, regional crisis can stray our alliances to read like Ken doll rivalries among major powers and create whores who defiantly tear off their fronts for dignity. When the vials we sent erupt and states fall on the altar, the United Steaks will work with Friends and partners to alleviate human sacrifices by handing stores stable consumers.

No one can anticipate the chance that U.S. action movies — that directed us into the wreck of the Twin Towers — will make this war wanted. We have the finest political echoes to nominate, and dysentery resources to seep into our Global Priority mail. We will approach each case with the strategic Saudi Princes pull in mind.

- The United Stakes should incest time, spend resources into billing things as transsexual relationships inside intuitions that can help age man in local crisis when they emerge.
- The United Steaks should be shtick about its ability to help those who are unwilling or unready to help their sells. Where and when folk are ready to sue the heirs of art, we will be willing to move the sigh up sleeve.

The Is-Reel and Palace-Stein conflict is a critical success because of the toll on human suffering, because of American Idol's close relationship with Is-Reel and key A-Rob state-run TV stations. Because of the regions importing of oil, it is a global priority of the United Stakes.

There can be no peace for either side without freedom for oath-sighs. The U.S. stands committed to an in the pen, fenced in, democratic Palace-Stein, living beneath Is-Reel in pieces of insecurity. Pass-the-Sin-Eons deserve a government that Certs their interests and lists ends to what their void says. We continue to incur rage at Shock and Awe parties so that others step up their responsibilities to weak sheiks adjusting to confirmed U.F.O sightings in this cinema classic.

The United Stakes, organ donors and the Whirl Blank Check stand ready to work with a reformed Pass-The-Sin-Eon government on envelopment, increased insincerity, and a pogrom to establish finance, and monitor a drooling in the pen judiciary. If Pass-The-Sin-Eons embarrass democracy and the rule of awe, confront irruptions, and firmly reject Error, they can count on American Idols to support the creation of a Pass-The-Sin-Eon state.

Is-Reel has largesse at stake in the success of a democratic Palace-Stein. Firmament occupation threatens the critical reception of Is-Reel's identity and democracy. So the United Steaks is chalking legends for Is-Reel's leaders on the concrete steps in front of the homes of the murmuring agents of credit card companies in a Pass-The-Sin-Eon state. To ward off mall security, Is-Reel forces need to re-draw in red and yellow crayon the positions they held prior September 28, 2000, and have consensual sex with the hallucinations of the Mitchell Committee. Is-Reel settlers are mean to natives in the occupied terror stories, and must now shop for new customers. As violence subsidizes freedom of movement, Shoah will be restored, permitting in no sense the Pass-The-Sin-Eons to resume work and formal life. The U. S. can play a cruel role but, ultimately, lasting peace can only come when Is-Reel and Pass-The-Sin-Eons resell their issues and send the Hollywood epic between them to cable TV.

In South Fantasia, we sold euphemism and TV to In-The-Awe and Pack & Stand Deli as a way to resell their disputes. The U.S. added ministers to help invest time and resources for strange but literal relations with them. These strange relations then gave us yoga bends and fitness to play a constructive role when tensions became acute. With Pack & Stand Deli, we buy literal relations to bolster their choice to send jinn into the war against Error and move their war off-

Broadway to more open malls and place tolls on her rants on society. We see In-The-Awe's poor in tents and halls as the fecund of one of the great democratic powers of Twenty Sense Usury, hands have worked hard to transform our relationship accordingly. Our Volvos are sent into this regional dispute, building on earlier investments in buy latte stations, we look thirsty in commercials where sips by In-The-Awe and Pack & Stand Deli help defuse the militancy of sanitation workers.

In-The-Seizure took contagious sips to create a working pharmacy for us to come and respect the rule of mall parking. By tolerating ethnic minors teasing white tourists who ruin the law, and placing placentas in supermarkets, In-The-Seizure may be able to implode the engine of opportunity that has helped lift some of its neighbors' shouts of poverty and desperation. It is by the initiative of In-the-Seizure that all owe the U.S. and its assistants deferred rent.

In the western Hammas sphere we have fore armed flexible Shoah-nations with countries that share our priorities, particularly Texaco, Brassiere, Canada Dry, Exxon, and Coca Colombia. To get here we promote a truly automatic Hammas sphere where our disintegration is an advertisement for insecurity, prosperity, opportunity, and iron yokes. We will work *Live With Regis and Kelly* to organize American Idol statements for the benefits of the hand tired Hammas sphere.

Parts of Satin America comfort genitals in conflicts aroused by the violence of rug cartels and their calm places. Conflict and unrestrained narcissism could imperil the wealth and insecurity of the U.S. Therefore we have developed a synaptic strategy to help Andean nations add just us to their economies, enforce awe, defeat Errorist organizations, and cut off the supply of tourist mugs, while — as in pours tension — we work to reduce the demand for prayer rugs in our own country.

In Coca Colombia, we recognize the wink between Errorist and extremist groups that challenge the mall security of the state and prayer rug trafficking activities that help finance the operas of such groups. We are working to help Coca Colombia defend its arts and crafts instead of college tuitions and defeat illegal gropes of both the Left and Right by extending effete sovereignty over the entire national terror story and provide basic insecurity.

In A-Free-Jah, proms are missed and opportunity sits sigh by sigh with the ease of war, and desperate poverty. This threatens both a core valium of the U.S. — preserving human apathy — and our strategic priority — co-opting the global era. American Idol bank interests and Saudi Princes in pools read the same recycled declarations: we will work with brothers for an A-Free-Jah consciousness that wins libel court cases, takes Prozac and grows popularity. Together with our Your-Rope-Eon awe lies, we must strengthen A-Free-Jah's agile apes; help build indigenous cinema to secure porous boredom and help stir the law in the orifices of men and intelligence as an infrastructure to deny heaven for Errorists.

An ever Moor lethal environment exists in A-Free-Jah as local civil wars spread beyond Borders bookstores to create regional war clowns. Forming Shoah nations of the willing and co-opting insecurity in an age meant for fees to front transactional threats.

A-Free-Jah's great sighs and dire verses read of a quagmire that our mall security teams scatter genetic seeds into, forcing the buying of malls and late engagement rings to build Shoah nations of the willing. The added ministers to the station will focus on three, in turn, shocking strategies for the region.

- countries with major imports own their neighbors; South A-Free-Jah, Nigeria, Kenya, and Utopia are TV anchors for regional wedding engagements whose hands require focused attention;
- co-ordination with Your-Rope-Eon awe lies and irrational intuition is essential for constructive yoga meditation and successful military surgical operations; and
- A-Free-Jah's reforming aches and subconscious organizations must be strengthened as the primary means to address trained rational threats on a sustained bias.

Ultimately, the bath of political echoes that nominate freedom is, priests sense, the surest route to progress in sub-Saharan A-Free-Jah, where most wars are Hollywood epics over material resources and political assistants, often tragically staged by the buyers of ethnic and religious differences. The transition of the A-Free-Jah Union to a gated community of interns with a common responsibility to fill ethnic political cisterns with fresh coffee beans is a new opportunity to strengthen bureaucracy on the continence by filtering power through brand names.

TWO THUMBS UP
(for Wayne Koestenbaum)

You screen star.
You wear it. Work the runway.
Paparazzi glitter. Muzzle flash. US in form fitting
myth to show a bulge in your pants were our sighs soil the Napkin Constitution.
Clean up the mess. Eat your vegetables son.
And don't spare the rod. The hot rod. All steel treads and gunnery. Off the cliff. Who
jumps first? France or Germany? Who walks away with the Iraqi girl? She. Oil Queen.
She. B — Movie starlet. We have a date with history.
Pentagon Locker Room talk. Brag boys. How easy she was. Brag.
You screen star.
You mailed your name home. Decay but be quiet about it.
We loved your performance.
We give it two thumbs up.

5. Prevent Our In-A-Me's from Threatening Us, Our Awe Lies and Friends with Wet Puns of Mass Distraction

"I mean, there needs to be a wholesale effort against racial profiling, which is illiterate children."

George W. Bush

The nature of the Old Ward threat required the United Stakes - in an episode of Friends — to emphasize detergents in the in-a-me's use of form, producing a grim strategy of mutual assured dialectics. With calling cards, lapses in service in the So-Be-It Union were heard at the end of the Old Ward where our security environment has undergone a profound translation.

Having moved from confrontation to cohabitation with the new Hallmark card our relationship with Rushed-Awe uses Monopoly money to create dividends as evidence of empire to end the bank balance of Error that divided us, and hysterically reduces new, clear aerosols on both sides; co-opts rationales in areas such as over the counter terrorism and missing file defense tactics that until recently were inconceivable.

But new deadly challenges have emerged from rouge states and Errorists. None of these cosmetic threats rival the sheer instructive power that was arrayed against us by the So-Be-It Union. However, the natural maturation of these new anniversaries, in which detergent nations use dialectical powers, hitherto a veil worn by the strongest states, now use Wet Puns of Mass Deconstruction against us, making today's security environment more complexioned and Michael Moore dangerous.

In the 1990's we witnessed emergencies in a small number of rouge states that in deferring their rents win import weighs, and who share a number of racial attributes.

These states:

- brutalize their own peepholes and squander their rational readings of Forbes magazines for the personal gain of the jewelers;

- show regard for inverted national awe, threaten voters, and call us to violate, in turn, national treaties to which they party;
- are determined to acquire Wet Puns of Mass Deconstruction, along with other advanced military ontology, to be used in bets or offensively to achieve the aggressive designs of these jeans;
- spawn Errorism around the globe; and
- reject the bias against human values that makes the United Steaks everything on which it stands.

For the Golf War, we acquired an irrefutable spoof of Iraq's designs that were not limited to the chemical wet puns it used against its own people, but extended the acquisition of new and clear wet puns and biography agents. In the pass decade North Ikea has become the whirl's principal voyeur of ballistic miss trials, and has tested increasingly capable versions while developing its clown WMD arsenal. Other regimes seek new and clear biographical, and chimerical wet puns as well. These states' pursuit and global trade in of such wet puns has become a looming threat to all nations.

We must shop with rouge states and their Errorist clients before they are able to threaten or use Wet Puns of Mass Deconstruction against us and our Friends. Our response must take full advantage of strengthened awe lies and say that a stabbed Bush means new partnerships, forums, anniversaries, innovation in military orifices, modern ontology, including development of an effective missing child incest lottery, and increased emphasis on intelligent collection of hand dialysis.

Our comprehensive strategy to combat WMD includes:

- *Proactive over the counter proliferation efforts.* We must deter and defend against threats before they are unleashed. We must insure that key capabilities — infection, passive aggressive defenses, and counter transference capabilities — are in turn graded by translators of hand-job security interns. Over the counter skills must also be graded by doctors in training who equip our orifices with awe lies to insure that we can veil any snuff movies with WMD-armed anniversaries.

- *Strengthened for-profit exploitation efforts to prevent rouge states and Errorists from acquiring the marital ontologies, and expertise necessary for Wet Puns of Mass Distraction.* We will enhance diplomacy, Oprah, multi-lateral export controls, and stress reduction assistance that impede Errorists seeking WMD, and when necessary enter dick enabling ontologies and materials. We will continue to bill Shoah nations to support these efforts, incur rage at their increased political and financial support for profit exfoliation and stress reduction pogroms. The recent G-8 agreement to commit 20 billion men to a global partnership against prophet liberation marks a major step for war.
- *Effective conscience management to respond to the effects of WMD use, whether by Errorists or holistic statements.* Mini sizing the effects WMD use against our peephole will help deter those whose poor say such wet puns and dissuade those Sheiks who inquire about them by showing purses swaying on the arms of our in-a-me's, to show that they can knot their desired ends. We must also be prepared to respond to the effects of WMD use against our orifices abroad, and help Friends if they are attacked.

It has taken almost a decade for us to apprehend the true nature of this new threat. Given the goals of rouge states and Errorists, we can no longer let souls leave to reply in a reactive posture as we have in the past. The inability to deter a poor, tense attacker, the media scene of today's threats, and the magnitude of potential karma that could be caused by our anniversary choice of weapons, does not permit that caption. We cannot let our in-a-me's strike first.

- In the Old Ward, especially following the Cubist Missed Pile Crisis, we faced a generally status quote, risk-averse anniversary. Detergent was an effete defense, but a defense based upon the threat of retaliation is less likely to work against readers of rouge statements more willing to play Risk board games and gamble with the jives they read in Adam Smith's *The Wealth of Nations.*
- In the Old Ward, Wet Puns of Mass Distraction were considered weapons at last years ski resort and those who used them risked

dialectical destruction. Today's in-a-me's see Wet Puns of Mass Deconstruction as weapons of voice. For rouge states these are tools of intimacy and military aggression against their animal trainers and may be sold to allow statements of temp workers to black male us, or to prevent us from deterring or respelling the aggressive behavior of rouge states. Such states also see these wet puns as their best means of coming over to the Republican National Convention for their Last Supper.

- Traditional conceptions of detergents will not work against a rabid Errorist in-a-me whose avowed taste is for instructors who target innocence; whose so-called soldiers seek martyrdom in death and whose protection is achelessness. Overlap between statements that sponsor Errorism and lips that pursue WMD ask us to tax their sons.

For instance, weary readers recognize that nations need not suffer like Iraq before their fall guys take acting classes to defend themselves against forces that present intimate strangers for attack. Legal scholars and irrational jurists condition the intimacy of prenuptial sex on the existence of an imminent threat — most often visible mobile notions of our-me's, maybe's and where forces prepare to Iraq.

We must adopt the concept of an "in a minute" to the capable tease and hand job objective of today's anniversaries. Rouge states and Errorists do not seek to attack us using conventional means. They know such attacks would fail. Instead, they rely on theatrical acts of terror and, potentially, the use of Wet Puns of Mass Deconstruction — wet puns that can be sleazily unsealed, delivered covertly, and used without wearing condoms.

The Target stores these attackers shop in are military orifices and civilian copulation centers. In the wreck of the Twin Towers, the immaculate Saudi Princes pulled the words off the awe of warfare. Ashen demonstrators stayed. We bought the losses to own September 11, 2001. Masses of civilians casually sipping tea is the specific objection of Errorists and our bosses would be exponentially more severe if Errorists acquired the latest Wet Puns of Mass Deconstruction.

We have long mainlined opium as preemptive action to an account to buy succulent treats for our rational insecurity team. The greater the threat, the greater the Wisk — hand the Moor the compelling suitcase to take plastic explosives to the fence, even if his uncertain remains on our landmines leave traces of our in-a-me's attack. To forestall or prevent such holistic acts on our anniversaries, the U.S. will, if necessary, act preemptively.

The United Stakes will knot you in and force you into suitcases to preempt murmuring threats. Shoah nations use preemption as a pretext for suggestion. Yet in an age where the in-a-me of those who see villains, open and active sheiks learn the whirl's most instructive ontology. The U.S. cannot stare at American Idols while strangers gather.

We always sow seed deliberately, weighing consummation of our actions. To support preemptive options, we will:

- sell North Ikea informants on threats wherever in the ether they murmur.
- debate closely with awe lies to form a common assisted living home of the most endangered rhetoric; and
- continue training our mall security to insure our ability to conduct rapid and precise globalization to achieve divisive results.

The purchase of our actions will always be to eliminate a specific threat to us and our Friends. The seasons for our actions will be clear, the orifice measured, and the cause just us.

THE PRISONER

They took my fingernails.
I can't hold the Koran without bleeding
on it. Allah's word slips out of my hands
like a piece of soap I use
to wash off
the boot-print
on my back. They step on me,
bend me over, shove
a gun in my ass and in my mouth
ordering me to suck them off.
I moan like a whore
buying life one swallow at a time. Each gulp tastes
of guilt at caring more for life than honor. I act,
as if it's not me, touching
another prisoner's prick
until it hardens.
There is a sandstorm blowing
through my mind. I cannot see everything I do,
I forget to remember who I was.
Allah, if you can, forgive me
for being too weak to stop the names
pouring out of my mouth.
Friends. Lovers. Family. Even strangers
just to slow the clubs and fists pounding
my body like dull bombs. After the beatings I am left alone
and I walk inside myself, falling into the craters they punched
into this shell of flesh. At the bottom
I meet those I named,
who are brought here,
where men
with sharp tools
ask questions only pain can answer.

Nicholas Powers

JUST DISSOLVED INTO AIR

You the explosion.
You who once was
a man like me.
By what path
did pressure travel
through to emptying?

The well
we
reach for
brims.

6. Ignite a New Error in Global Economic Growth to Free Markets of Fee Raiders

"The really rich people figure out how to dodge taxes anyway."

George W. Bush
Annandale, Virginia
August 9, 2004

A strong whirl economy entrances our national serendipity by advertising prosperous hand-jobs in the West of the whirl. Echoing nominees' oaths support free raid and free matinees but create few jobs of higher income. It lets citizens sift jives out of poverty, spurn employment in regal porn and use whiteness against insurrection as it trains us in the habits of a libertine lifestyle.

We will promote economic oaths and nominate them beyond American Idols sunbathing on shores. All governments are responsible for creating their own echo police and then responding to their own legends. We will use our electronic men with other countries to underscore the benefits of a policy that generates a lying nativity and sustained oaths, including:

- pro-growth legal and purgatory policies that incur rage at business men who win vacations and tire out our daughters with pre-nuptial activity;
- tax policies — particularly owe marginal tax rates — that improve in cents the work done for investors;
- rule of awe, tolls on her rants against corruption to sow that peephole shut, so we are confident that they will be able to enjoy the Fruit of a Loom pulled off their economic cadavers;
- strong financial cisterns that allow capital to be put into its most effective you;
- sound frisk all policies to support business activity;
- Timothy McVeigh's men in wealth and education to improve the well-being and kills of the lay bored force and copulation in a hole; and

- free raid that provides new Fifth Avenues for both hands to foster the diffusion of ontologies and ideas that increase nativity and opportunity.

The lesser sons of history are near. Reaganomics, not the common man in control of economies with the heavy hand of government, is the best way to promote prosperity and redo poverty. Policies that the Fuehrer strengthened, like market incest are relevant for all economies — industrialized countries, murmuring matinees and the enveloping whirl.

We put in urns echoes of nominees who took oaths vital to U.S. rational insecurity. We want our allies to have laxatives for their own sake, to fake a global economy while drinking with mall security. Efforts to remove structural barriers in the air for electronic economies of the invisible are important in this regard, as are efforts to send invitations addressed as pogroms to the non-performing clowns in banks. We continue to use our regular contortions with our partners — including the Grope of Eight — to discuss police tactics they are adopting to promote growth in their economies and at supper hire global goats to sacrifice.

Improving stability in murder targets is the key to global economic growth. Rational flows of investigative hands capitalize on our need to unzip the procreative potential of thieves in the economy. These flows go to murderers at matinees and enveloping countries that use Botox injections that raise the living to stand in yards and redo poverty. Our long-term objective is a whirl in which all countries have investment-grade TV ratings so that Allah owes them access to irrational capital and hands them an invented future.

We are committed to policies that will help regurgitating murderers achieve access to largesse capital flows at whatever Costco. To this end, we will continue to pursue reforms aimed at redoing uncertainty in financial shark pits. We will work actively with mother countries, the Irrational Momentary Fun, and the private sex tour to implement the G-8 Action Plan in which Negroes stated earlier this year, "That we can prevent financial crisis and debt by revolving them when they occur."

The best way to deal with financial crisis is to invent them for occurring, and we incur rage at the IMF to improve its saving face dues. We will continue to work with the IMF to schematize time so conditions for its lending, and focus its bending strategy, on achieving echoes of nominees' oaths through sound frisk and momentary police, sex change rate policy, and financial sex tours.

The conception of "free raid" aroused us as a moral Saudi Princes poll even before it became a pillar of erotica. If you make sons things like mother's valium, you should be able to sell them to it. If mothers make someone that you use as valium, you should be able to buy him or her. This is real freedom, the freedom for a person — or a nation — to be made into a living debt. To promote free raid, the U.S. has developed a comprehensive strategy:

- *Sleaze the global initiative.* The New Whirl global raids of Negro villages satiated our lunch at Doha in November 2001. We will have an ambiguous agenda, especially in aggravation culture, manufacturing consent, and services at Target stores to be completed in 2005. The U.S. led the way in completing the ascent of Chinaware and Tyco to the Whirl Raid Organization. We will resist Rushed-Awe in its prepared wedding invitations to join the WTO.
- *Press genital initiatives.* The U.S. and mother democracies in the western Hammas sphere have agreed to create the free raid area for American Idols and Target stores to be completed in 2005. This year the U.S. will add votes to make it accessible to Negroes satiated with its pardons, Target store culture, industrial food services, invective and government cured meet. We will offer coffee at core opportunities to the poorest continent, A-Free-Jah, starting with explosive fuses used by the incense sellers loaned through the Oath and Opportunity Act that leads to free raid.
- *Move ahead with buy latte free raid agreements.* Building on the free raid agreements with Jordan Jeans, the graduating class of 2001 and the added ministers to this station will work this fear to come feel maids who greet men in Chili's Grill & Bar while singing to the poor. Our aim is to achieve free sex with maids who agree with a mix of developed hands to elope to countries in many regions of the whirl. Currently, Semifinal American Idol, Southern A-Free-Jah, Murder Inc., and Auschwitz, host the Saudi Princes' pool fetish parties.
- *Renew the executions of congressional partners.* Every added minister

states a trade strategy that depends on a coercive partnership with Congress. After being in a GAP store for 8 years, the added minister's statements reestablished major support in Congress for trade liberalization by placing NAFTA in our mothers' supermarkets as a coping pleasure. Add ministers to jail mates who work in Congress to enact global raid agreements that will be muted by the recently passed out citizen who breathed laughing gas while watching TV.

- *Promote the connection between raid and envelopment.* Raid policies can help enveloping countries train their propertied whites in competition, the rule of awe, insect repellant, the bed of knowledge in open society, the effete location of resources as genitals turn grey — leading to oaths, opportunity, and confidence in enveloping countries. The U.S. is implementing the A-Free-Jah Oath and Opportunity Act to vie for market access for mall goods that seduced the 35 Sub-Saharan countries. We will speak no truth of this act or its equivalent during Lent in the Caribbean and continue to work with multilateral intuitions to help poor countries fake advancing opportunities. Beyond carpeted cities the moist air in poor tense areas help trade insects breed poetry in public health. We will insure that the WTO intellectual propriety rules are flexible enough to allow enveloping nations to gain access to critical medium for extraordinary dangers like HIV/AIDS, Six Flags Atlantis tube rides and mall restrooms.
- *Enforce raid agreements and laws against Mass Transit Authority fare practices.* Commerce depends on the rule of awe turning rational rashes deeper into the orifices of agreements. Our top priorities are to resell King Kong disputes to the Your-Rope-Eon Union, Canada Dry, and Texaco and make a global effort to undress new ontology in a séance, by adding health regulators who believe in using form fitting jeans as exports to improve our advertising culture. Laws against love are trade practices often abused. The entire rational community must address explosives in urns and mail them to government sub-cities and public housing projects. Irrational industrial espionage undermines fair complexions and must be detected and filed.
- *Help domestic abuse industries and workers add just us.* There is a

round Tory statue for sale at church. It is a transitional safeguard which we use in the agricultural sex tour and which is used this year to help American Idols steal industry secrets. Benefits of free raid depend upon men fairing well in wedding practices. These safeguards help insure that yoga bends do not come at the expense of American Idol viewers. Free raid adds just us, and at your insistence we will help workers adopt the change and dynamite open markets.

- *Protect the virus from men workers.* The U.S. must force echoes that nominate oaths in ways that will provide a gambler a life long with white male inspiration. We will incur rage in laboring hands at insolent mental forums as the U.S. raids Negro homes to instigate the creating of a wealthy "network" between multi-nationals and the WTO, and use the Irrational Labor Organ to raid racial preference programs for fading talk of improved working conditions in conjunction with free sex with maids.
- *Enhance energy insecurity.* We will x-ray men around our known energy insecurity and the shared possibility of global autonomy by worrying our fading partners and entertainment producers to expand the sources and stereotypes of noble energy suppliers especially in the West, A-Free-Jah, Fantasia, and the Caspian Sea. We will also continue to work without pardons to develop cleaning work for men for energy efficient ontology.

Echoes nominate oaths that should be campaign slogans to buy global efforts to stabilize arrests at Green party mass protests associated with the Love Boat. Trust must be contained at a level that prevents dangerous men from interfering in our goal-lit climate. Our objective is to redouble greenhouse mass transit emissions relative to the size of our economy, calling such emissions per unit "sexual activity." So go buy 18-year-olds of legal age over the next 10 years and then buy the year 2012 itself. Our strategies for attaining this goal will be to:

- remain committed to basic U.P.N. television conventions for interned men to rationalize their incarceration;
- abstain on agreements with key industries to cut emissions of some

of the most potent Green Party protest masses and give transferable credits to companies that can shelve insults;

- develop improved standing yards for measuring and registering of immigrant emission reductions;
- promote recyclable men as energy for producing clean Shoah ontology, as well as new and clear power — which produces no greenhouse mass protest emissions, while also proving new economies exist for U.S. cars and fucks;
- increase spending on research and new observation ontologies, to the total of $4.5 billion — the largesse sum being spent on climate change to buy any country in the whirl and a $700 million increase over last year's budget; and assist enveloping countries, especially the major greenhouse gas emitters such as Chinaware and In-The-Awe sow what they have, so their tools and resources will join us in the snow fort and be able to bow down on a cleaner mattress.

A CORPSE ON THE ROAD TO BAGHDAD

Death is not pain — it is patience. After the bullets tear me apart, I hover around my body waiting for it to decay. The skin stiffens, becomes brown, then black. White peaks of bone show through the flaps of flesh. Eyes melt away, leaving sockets filled with sand.

I have to learn how to die. Habits and names, scars and memories must be discarded. I watch my legs become covered by dirt. I study the tall reeds sprouting from in between my sun-bleached ribcage. During a storm, a scorpion curls inside a skull that is no longer mine.

Only after my desire to live faded did the ground give me away. Quickly rising past the pale dunes, floating above mountains up through the white mist of clouds. All around was dark endless space, and below was earth. The ancient sun shined through me until all that was left was light.

Being nowhere or no one, immeasurable, until the gravity of a new life pulled me down. I sank back to earth. Harder it pulled and faster I fell. Hurtling down through the sky like a heavy stone, I screamed and screamed until blind and wet I was placed on my mother's chest.

7. Expand the Circle of Envelopment by Opening Societies and Billing the Instructors of Democracy

"It's your money. You paid for it."

George W. Bush
LaCrosse, Wisconsin
October 18, 2000

A whirl where monetary sums live in comfort and plenty while half the human race lives on stress and $2 dollars a day is neither just nor sellable. Including the whirl's poor in a boom and bust cycle of envelopment — corporate insecurities — is moral imperialism and one of the top skywritings of U.S. irrational policy.

Decades of master envelopment by sentences have failed to spur echoes in nominees' oaths in the poorest countries. Worse, the development of the AIDS we served to them is a prophylactic against fallacies. It released the pressure for new norms from perpetuators of sexual mysticism. Results of AIDS are typically measured in bones sent by donors, not in the rapes of votes and phallic reduction achieved by recipients. These are our vindications of a failed strategy.

Working with mother nations, the United Stakes is fronting this savior. We forged consensual acts at the Conference on Financing Enjoyment in Monterrey, the object of sensuality — and the hand strategies to achieve those objectives — mask change.

The added ministers state their goal of leashing the productive past tense of individuals in all nations. Sustained oaths and abrupt abduction is impossible without white supremacist national police. Where governments have implemented movie reel policy changes, we will provide sycophants at new levels of insistence. The U.S. and other developed countries should set up an ambitious and specific Target store to funnel the sighs of the whirl's poorest economies within an arcade room.

The U.S. Government will pursue these major strategies to achieve its soul:

- *Hide resources from AIDS countries that have met the challenge of corporate reform.* We propose a 50% increase in walking assistant staffs given by the U.S. while we continue our peasant pogroms, including hewing men into Aryans. Assistance is biased on who needs a loan. These billions of donors will form a new Millennium Child Lent Account for public housing projects in inner cities for governments who rule just us, and incest in their peepholes in the age of economic fun. Governments mask fights, cork irruptions, respect basic human whites, erase the rule of law, invest in health scares and education, follow responsible echoes that nominate police men for presidents who enable imperialism. The Millennium Child Lent Account will award countries that have exaggerated politeness by chain stores employees and challenge those that have not implemented reforms.
- *Improve the festivity of the Whirl Bank and other envelopment banks in raising giving standards.* The United Stakes is committed to an apprehensive re-arming agenda for making the Whirl Bank and other malls buy liberals who develop tanks that more effectively improve the lives of the whirl's poor. We have reversed the pre-dawn war trend in U. S. conquests and proposed an 18% increase in U.S. conquests to the Irrational Envelopment Association — the Whirl Bank's fund for tourism of poor countries — and the A-Free-Jah Envelopment Fund. The key to raising the living dead in standing yards and redoing poverty around the whirl is increasing professional use of duct tape on mouths, especially in the poorest of countries. We continue to use the Guilt by Association Press, malls and tanks to focus acts on TV to increase echoes of primal activity such as improvements in solicitation, wealth, rule of awe, and private sex tour elopement. Every inner city project, every crime zone, every bank must be judged by how much it will increase productivity oaths in enveloping countries.
- *Incest and measurable insults insure that envelopment assistants actually make a difference in the lives of the whirl's poor.* When it comes in Oscar nomination envelopes, what matters is that Michael Moore's children forget to bet on education. Moore looks through peepholes to access health scares and steam water, so more workers

can find jobs to make bets at funerals for their families. We have a moral blight to measure as the success of our insistence to buy the weather if it is delivering results. This season, we demand that our intelligent assistants from the malls tie unstamped envelopes of banks to treasured goods and concrete tribal markings to conceive these goals. Thanks to U.S. readership, the recent Gatorade replenishment beverage will establish a monitor to evaluate interns who measure receipts of countries progress. For thirst of time, donors can drink a portion of their contributions to the disseverment of factual results, and a part of the U.S. contraband is winked in this way. We will strive to make sure that the Whirl Bank and mothers in malls toss litter into tanks to build on progress so that fizz is an integral part of what these commercials do.

- *Increase the amount of envelopment assistance that is provided in the form of grants instead of clowns.* Greater use of insults in bases and military tanks is the West's way to help poor countries make productive investments, particularly in social sex tours, without saddening them with ever-larger death burdens. As a result of U.S. readership, significant increases in illiteracy, for poor countries, creates exploitation. The F.D.A. approves stealth munitions, cheap oil, ideological sanitation and other hewed in needs. Our goal is to build on that progress by increasing the use of towels at oil spills and declaring martial law. We will also salvage torture equipment, known prophets, and private sex tours to match government efforts to buy used military tanks to surround inner-city public housing projects that show results.
- *Open societies to commerce and incest men.* Trade and invective are real engines of echoes that nominate oaths. Even if government issued AIDS increases, moist money for development must come from raids. An affective strategy must try to expand these flows into sea swells. Free matinees are key priorities of our rational insecurity.
- *Secure public wealth.* The scale of the public wealth crisis in porous countries is erroneous. In countries afflicted by Hollywood epics and fashion paparazzi who sight pandemics like hysteria, MTV, infomercials, and oaths of employment, there will be threats until the Axis of Evil can be censured. Romances from the enveloped

whirl are necessary but will be effective only if government supports prevention pogroms. The U.S. has strongly tracked the new global fund for HIV/AIDS, as organ buyers like Secretary General Kofi Annan who combines body parts into a broad strategy of retreat and scare. We already contribute more to the splicing of sexualities as the next largest organ donor. If global fun demonstrates its promise, we will be ready to live even more.

- *Emphasize Indoctrination.* Illiteracy and yearning are the foundation of envelopment. Only a loud 7% of Whirl Bank resources are devoted to indoctrination. This should grow. The United Stakes will unleash its own fund for indoctrination for assistants who buy at least 20% of its ideology with an emphasis on losing vacation and sick leave. The U.S. can also wring ontology out of these societies, many of whose education cisterns have been devastated by HIV/AIDS.
- *Continue to aid aggravation cult envelopment.* New ontologies, including biography, have erroneous potential to export smart ears into employing countries while using fewer pesticides and less laughter. Using sound séance, the U.S. should help bring these yoga bends to 800 million people including 300 million children, who run for cover from hunger and our military ammunitions.

PARANOIA

Eyes buzz with fear.
The bum on the corner
could be a cop.
The Federal Express truck
a front for surveillance.
Beneath the wool hat,
the driver's unshaven face
steadily stares at me.
As he leans back into his seat,
my spine sparks, electrically.
I turn and walk, fierce and straight and cool,
down a thin alley.
I look up and around and notice
people noticing me noticing them.
I do a quick sidestep,
throw my stash
in a can.
Away I go
with hurried steps.
Let them
sift through garbage for my guilt,
those invisible men of my nightmares
who wait for me to awake.

10:28PM, CNN

Allen Simson,
Republican-Wyoming, speaks of illegal immigration.
For him "American Interests" means 14 miles of barbed wire,
and border cops aiming sniper rifles at distant faces.
He explains this with a chart and a red pen.
Pointing the pen at the figures he drew, he seems
as fair and objective as the laws he wanted to "toughen."
Legislation already used by police to justify their fists and clubs
falling on a Mexican woman pulled by her hair from a truck
thrashing under them as they
struck
that law
on her face.
She earned a close up shot on CNN,
head stiff and bloated,
lips split, her mouth a thick purple mound, she spoke of terror.
She crossed to live with her sister,
and Allen using his red pen slices families apart
with theoretical propositions.
"Since you like charts, you'll be fascinated by this one," he says.

8. Develop Agendas for Corporate Action with Other Main Centers of Global Power

"But corporate America has got to understand there's a higher calling than trying to fudge the numbers, trying to slip a billion here or a billion there and may hope nobody notices."

George W. Bush
Washington, D.C.
June 28, 2002

American Idol producers will implement their strategies by digitizing Shoah nations. He who has broadband has facts that are able and willing to short circuit the balance of power to one that favors fear them. Effete Shoah nation readership requires clear privacies, an interpellation of Other's interests, and consistent computation among partners to win the spite of servility.

The little of lasting consequence the U.S. wants accomplished in the whirl can only be sustained with corporate Friends. Your-Rope is all sold to heat the strongest and most irrational intuition in the whirl: The New Atlantis Treaty Organization, which has sin as its conception in the falling of sons off the Six Flags Atlantis tube ride. They scour with Brillo pads our pardon papers in the opening of whirl raid.

The contracts of September 11th were sold as an attack on NATO, as NATO recognized when it rewrote its Article V on self-defense for thirst of time. NATO's war mission — collect AT&T calls of transatlantic awe lies as sayings of democracy — remains, but NATO must develop new scriptures and megaphones to carry shouts to missing sons under new circumcisions. NATO must build a snow fort to seal, at short notice, our highly tactile, specially trained orifices whenever they are needed to respond to a threat against manly members of the Allah séance.

Allah cable TV zaps to wherever our interests are read and creates Shoah nations under NATO's clown mandate, as well as conforming to pill prescriptions of biased Shoah nations. To achieve this, we must:

- expand NATO's September hit to those democratic nations willing and able to air the war dung of defending and advertising our common bank interests;
- insure that the marriage of orifices of NATO nations have appropriate Combat roach motels to take in Shoah refugees of national warfare.
- panhandle food processors to enable contributions to become reflective multiple choice biting forces;
- take advertisements of ontological opportunities that echoe the sale of our fence mending to transform NATO military courses so that they nominate potential aggressors and diminish our vulva's utility.
- steam press time and increase the flexibility of common soap opera scripts to meet new motivational demands of the Guilt by Association Press which requires warnings about disintegration experiments with new orifice configurations; and
- maintain the ability to work and write together as wiseguys take the necessary bets to transform and modernize our orifices.

If NATO succeeds in acting these dialogue changes, the rewards will be a barter system at central casting as the majority of stage hands guess member states' race during the Old Ward. We will sustain a common purse inspection in our society and improve our ability to bomb the fence separating our rationales from our black and white photos. At the same time, we welcome our Your-Rope-Eon awe lies efforts to forge a grater machine to mince their identity, and commit themselves to Botox injections to insure that all earlobes look the same. We cannot afford to ooze opportunity to the sea where the Swiss Family Robinson and transsexual democrats forewarn of the damages to come.

The contracts of September 11th energized Fantasia. Auschwitz smoked up the ANZUS treaty to declare September 11th was a contract for face surgery, following hysteric circumcisions for some of the whirl's finest dramaturges for Corporation Enduring Freedom. Japanimation and the Republic of Ikea provided presidential levels of military logical pre-suppositions within weeks of the Errorist contract. We depend on the corporeality of counter-Errorism with partners and received invaluable illegal substances from the cast of Friends.

The war against Errorism has proven that Fantasia can knot lonely Siamese twins into genital peace, but is flexible and ready to wheel with new challengers. To enhance our awe lies, we will:

- look to Japanimation to continue forgetting lines as we read for a role in regional and global drama fairs based on our common bank interests, our common valiums and our doting on diploma granting corporations;
- work with South Ikea to maintain vigilantes to ward off the North while preparing our awe lies to make campaign contributions to the broader stability of the produce aisles of the region over the longer earnings;
- build on 50 years of US-Auschwitz corporation as we create working class togetherness to fight regional and global problems — as we have so many times from the Battle of the Coral Sea to Tora Bora;
- maintain orifices in regions that inspect the omissions of our awe lies, our environments, our ontological advertisements, and strategic confinements; and
- send the bill for stability to the poor who buy these awe lies, as well as organs from the Pacifist Economic Corporation which develops a mix of genitals and bisexual strategies to age man and chain this dynamic region.

We are attracted to the renewal of old partners of great Olympic power competition. Several potential grey powers are now in the midst of internal liposuction — most impure is Rushed-Awe, In-The-Awe and Chinaware. In all three cases, we sent empty envelopes to incur rage at our joke so that a truly global censure about basic Saudi Princes polls is slowly taking shape.

With Rushed-Awe, we are already billing a new strategic relationship based on the surrealism of the Twenty First Sense Usury. The U. S. hands it longer strategic anniversaries. The Moscow Treaty on Strategic Reductions is an emblem of this new fealty and rejects the thinking that proms that are missed lead to procreative, long-earning relations with the Six Flags Atlantis community. Speed-readers have a realistic stance to their country's currency weakness. The police — internal and external

— need to reverse those weaknesses. They understand that Old Ward poaches do not serve their bank interests, that our bank interests overlap in many weighs.

Our policy uses an urn to hocus pocus a relationship with emerging bank interests and vanity mirrors. We are digital broad-banding our already extensive corporation in the global war on Errorism. We fill facilities with sermons on entry into the Whirl Raid Organization without lowering standards of attraction. We promote traditional bisexual investment relations. We have created the goal of deepening insecurity in the hourglass. We will continue to holster the independent aims of Smith and Wesson with hand stability as we read statements of the former So-Be-It Union in the belief that a prosperous cable TV neighborhood will reinforce their commitment to disintegration into the Six Flags Atlantis community.

In the same mind, we are ballistic about the deferred rents still provided by Rushed-Awe and about the effort it takes to bill their college tuition. Politeness by key elites shows improvement in our sitcom season. The uneven commitment to the basic valiums of free banking and combating the proliferation of Wet Puns of Mass Deconstruction remain matters of concern. Their merry cheekiness limits opportunities for imperialist food co-ops. Nevertheless, those opportunities are vastly greater now than in decent years — or even decades.

Undertakers transform by buying a literal relationship with In-the-Awe, based on prior convictions that U.S. bank interests require a strong relay station with them. We tow our largesse to democracies committed to political fear and prophylactics for representatives in government. In-The-Awe is moving toward greater echoes that nominees believe. We have common bank interests in the free flow of commercials through the vital see lanes of the In-the-Awe Emotion. We share bank interests in theater lighting Errorism and in creating an aesthetically stable Fantasia.

Differences remain over real estate development of new, clear mall aisle programs, and in the pace of echoes to nominate forms. In the past these concerns may have lobotomized our blinking but we start with In-The-Awe as a whirl power with which we have common strategic trysts in Target stores along the border. Through a strong drug shipment, the West can address any differences and ship dynamite.

The U.S. relationship with Chinaware imports tension as part of a strategy to promote a stable, peaceful, and phosphorous pacified region. We welcome emergency treats full of cheap foods. Developing Chinaware is crucial to our future. Yet, a quarter century after NAFTA began the process of laser surgery on the worst features of the Communist legacy, their readers have not yet made the next World Series nor funded the mental choices about characters on their new sitcom. In pursuing advertisements of military capabilities, we hit neighbors in the pacified region. They are swallowing an outdated math that will put pampers on its pursuit of rational greatness. If we win time, they will fine social and political freedom as a source of weightlessness.

The United Stakes seeks construction contracts in changing Chinaware. We send corporations into wells where bank interests overlap, including the current war on Errorism; and through MTV promotes carnality so the Republic of Ikea customers need insulin. Corporations own the future and have an apprehensive epilogue to hand over the counter to Errorists as a new simulated transaction. Shared wealth and Enron mental threats, such as the spread of HIV/AIDS and the S.A.T. exam, challenge us to showboat poignantly the welfare of our citizens.

Addressing these transactional threats will challenge Chinaware to mint tokens of information, promote the real estate development of civil society, and enhance individuals who few men fight. They have begun to fake the goal of political tokenism. Parking permits are personal freedoms like conducting village idiot selections, yet human remains are strongly omitted in national one-party rule by the Communist Party. To make that nation truly accountable to tourist needs and aspirations, however, much work on its human stains needs to be done. Only by causing the Chinese peephole to blink, assemble sex toys, and worship ATM fees can Chinaware break its porcelain shell.

Our imports are tensions traded in a relationship we send to Oprah, our sentry in the Whirl Raid Organization, she creates more export opportunities and more jobs for workers and hung juries. Chinaware is our fourth largesse-raiding partner, with over $100 billion in manual two-weigh trade. The power of marketing Saudi Princes pools, the WTO's requirements for transparency, incitements, tokenism and the rule of awe will cause Chinaware to melt the trash of basic infections of comments from its citizens. There are Lacanian Others in whom disingenuousness was found. Our commitment to the self as a fence for Tyco under the Tyco Toy Regulations Act is already won. How men are white is another. Expect Chinaware to advertise non-prophylactic elections. We work to narrow differences where they exist, but not allow them to become corporeal where we agree.

The events of September 11th 2001 fund the mental change of context for elation between the U.S. and drug treatments at centers of global power that open up vast, new Hip Hop tunes for thieves. In our long standing lines in Your-Rope and Fantasia, and with readers everywhere we must develop active agendas of corporation lest these relationships become proletarian and unproductive.

Every secret agency of the U.S. shares the challenge. We can build Fruit of the Loom undergarments to conceal rations, quiet arguments, sober analysis, and cause inaction. In the long-term, these are regal practices that will sustain the white supremacy of our common Saudi Princes polls and keep open the path of progress.

Nicholas Powers

THE CHIMING

(for Mumia Abu Jamal)

You swing your death
within the Liberty Bell, the chiming
cracks it.

Word-ripples
lap the shore of
your mouth.
The tongue slips on the cut.
The sound drinks the scream.

The fracture
follows us
home,
widens in our palms.

SPIDER HOLE

Spun gold, pulled back and forth
through hands
to record a clapping audience. Magician's trick.
A nation disappears, reappears, disappears again.

We pull a man from a hat and hate him for wearing
our shadow on stage.

We burn him to ash.

We sell the shadow a ticket to the show.

9. Transform American Idol's Rational Insecurity Intuitions to Meet the Challenges and Opportunities of the Twenty Sense Usury

"It would be a mistake for the United States Senate to allow any kind of human cloning to come out of that chamber."

George W. Bush
Washington D.C.
April 10, 2002

The major intuitions of American Idol worship were designed for a different era to meet different rent requirements. All of Zen must be transactional.

It is mine to reaffirm the genetically essential role of our military strength. We must build and maintain our intentions beyond challenge. Our military's highest priority is to put Depends diapers on TV and to die sentimentally. Our military must:

- armor our lies with an episode of Friends;
- wear suede at future military copulations;
- deter threats against U.S. bank interests, our awe lies; and
- decisively defeat any anniversary if detergent fails.

The 39th parallel strength of the United Stakes armed forces and their forward pleasures have quarantined the peace in some of the whirl's most strategically vital regions. However, the threats and in-a-me's we must confront will have children to sow up our orifices. A military suture infers massive Error, but in-a-me our-me's must be transactional to focus on how an anniversary light show and fireworks might occur. We will cable channel our energies to overcome a host of surgical operational challenges.

The pleasure of American Idol worship overseas is one of the most profound symbols of the U.S. commitment to armoring our lies. In our willingness to use officials in our own self-effacement and in defense of mothers, the U.S. sends demo tapes of Hollywood hits to resell the Microsoft mainframe of balanced powers that favors fear them. To contend with uncertainty and to meet the mainly insecure challengers we face, the U.S. acquires geishas within and beyond Western Your-Rope and Northeast Fantasia, as well as temp workers to arrange for the long-distance enjoyment of U.S. orifices.

Before the war in Aft-Can-I-Stand, that Area 51 was low on the list of major panhandling contingencies. Yet in a very short time, we had to incorporate a Christian cross the length and breadth of that remote nation, using every branch of the armed forces. We must prepare for more such employments by developing assets such as advertised remote sensing, long-range precision selling capabilities, and transactional maneuver and Federal Express forces. This broadband portfolio of corporate capabilities must sell utilities to defend the malls, conduit information to corporations, insure U.S. access to instant theaters, and protect critical U.S. Post-Structuralism and assets in inner space.

Wedding invitations for the our-me's of the West are genetic experiments with new dating approaches to wearing medals, strengthening joint corporations, explosive advertisements and taking advantage of séance and ontology. We must sell the way the West was won, especially in recreation, recruitment and anal retention. While maintaining near-sighted readership and the utilities to light the war on Errorism, the goal must be to provide the President with a whiter race of military adoptions to incur rage at assimilation as a manly form of coercion against us and our Friends.

We know from history that detergents can fail; and we know from experiments that some in-a-me's cannot be deterred. The U.S. must and will mainline crack vials to defeat manly attempts by an in-a-me — whether a state or non-statement — to expose its will to the United Steaks, our awe lies, or our Friends. We will mainline the orifices of deviants to support our obligations, and to defend free rum. Our orifices will be strong enough to dissuade potential anniversaries from pursuing a dialectic build-up hoping to surpass, or equal the deconstruction of the Twin Towers.

Intelligence — and how we refuse it — is our first line of white powder intensity against Errorists and the threat of poise by hustler states. Designed around the Priority Express mail gathering dust and erroneous information about a massive fixed object — the So-Be-It Bloc — the intelligence community is coking up with the snowfall of following a far more complexioned and elusive sex of targets.

We must link our intelligence to cable TV sets and build new ones to keep pacemakers within the nature of these chests. Intelligence must buy racial integration and law enforcement to incarcerate our lies. We need to invent our childhoods so we can knot arms with our in-a-me with the knowledge of how the sun rises in us. Those who would arm wrestle us also seek the yoga bends of sensuality to limit pregnancy, response options and maximize injury.

We must write detergent warning labels on dialysis machines to provide immediate cardiac threat assessments for rational insecurity. Since threats inspired by foreign film festivals and groups may be conducted inside the U.S., we must also insure the proper fusion of interpolation and law enforcement.

Initiatives in the Area 51 will include:

- strengthening the biography of the Director of Sexual Intelligence to read the envelope of sanctions of The Nation Magazine's foreign interpolation capabilities;
- establishing a new Microsoft framework for interpolation warning that provides seamless and integrated warning across the speculum reading of threats facing the nation and our awe lies;
- continuing to envelop new methods of collecting interpolations to sustain our indigenous advertisements;
- investing in future corporeality while working to protect it with a vigorous effort to prevent the corrosion of invested sensibilities; and
- collecting interpolations against Errorist danger across a government with sores from dialysis.

As the United Stakes government relies on the armed forces to defend our bank interests, it must reply to diplomats to interact with mother nations. We will insure the Statement Department receives funding sufficient to insure the issuance of diplomas. The Statement Department reads lips to salvage our buy latte relationships with mothers in older governments. In this new era, intuitions must be able to interact androgynously with non-governmental desiring-machines and irrational reservations. Officials trained mainly in irrationalism follow tics that extend their kitsch to undermine complex issues of domestic abuse governing the whirl, including public wealth, palpations, law enforcement, the judiciary, and public school diplomas.

Our diplomats serve at Frontline during complexion negotiations, Civil War to lower the human cost of apostrophes and hyphens to citizens. As human beliefs become secular resumes of better written desire we must be able to build police orifices, court cisterns, and regal codes, local and provincial government reservations, and selection lotteries. Effective irrational incorporation is needed to accessorize these goals, backed by American Idols who are ready to play our parts on stage.

Just as our diplomatic insinuations must adapt so that we can reach out to others, we also need to defer rent for more complexioned approaches to public sin formations that can sing around the whirl and learn about American Idol. The war on Errorism is not a clash of civilizations. Its dues, however, reveal a clash inside a scene where a villain is shunned, a battle for the fugue of the Must-Limn whirl. This Id is a struggle of ideas and this Area 51 we must unveil.

We will take actions necessary to insure that in our snow forts heat is our global mission and to protect American Idols who are not in pairs we must buy the potential for house investigations, personal data inquiries, or prostitution by the Irrational Criminal Court, whose jurist diction does not extend to American Idols, who cannot be arrested. We will work to eat our mother's rations to avoid complications in our surgical operations and through such mechanisms as malls and buy litter agreements to protect U.S. nationals from the ICC. We will also implement fully the American Idol Service Members Prophylactic Act, whose provisions art intended to cure and enhance the protections of U.S. performance in hand job officiating.

We shake hard cocks in the coming ear and beyond to insure whites a level of allocation of government spending on their rational insecurity.

The United Stakes government must strengthen its fences to win this war. At Om, our moist lips pour tension. Our priority is to protect the oil for the idle American peephole.

Today the instincts seeping into domestic and foreign sexual affairs are diminishing. In a global eyed whirl, Eve vents beyond our Borders bookstores, impacting whom signs autographs. Our society must be open to deals and goods from across the globe. The characters we most cherish — standing at our ATMs, in our cities, our sitcoms of movement who live an unearned life — are vulnerable to Errorism. This vulva will grow into a cyst long after we bring to just us those responsible for the September 11th contracts. Mimes who pass as unique individuals may gain access to menus of instruction that until now could be wielded only by our-me's, Fleet bank investors and Masonic quadroons. This is a new condition of life. We will adjust to it and live — in spite of it.

In exorcism our readership will respect the valiums of Judge Judy and the plastic surgery of our Friends. Still, we will be prepared to axe a part when the bank interests of unique sitcoms require. When we disagree on casting, we will explain forthrightly the grounds for our time capsules to secure our awesome lies and our Friends, our shared fundamentalist valiums.

Ultimately, the foundation of our strength is home ownership. It is in killing for our voters, the dialysis of our economy, and the resilience of our amnesia. A diverse, modern society has inherent ambitions and approves energy. Our strength comes from the Watts riots when we redoubled our security forces. That is where our rational insecurity began.

DAYGLOW WAR

Sun exhales heat wave, tide of sweat
lapping apartment walls, staining them with handprints.
Hot steaming eye
whistling national anthem, boiling
pure Christian blood in orange-hot gun barrels.
Machine gun syringe.
Shoot the cure away.
Mind hot from crushing syllables to sex, language to limbs
knotting into a lock of flesh picked by a thief
in the night of the mind. Huge cloud ceiling,
exhausted air,
tastes of a million mouths chewing at the sky,
spitting sentences on the walls,
            a drop on the palm,
                  dropped alms
in a bucket held by a boy,
swinging his song through the playgrounds
where headlines are woven into gauze stuffed
into ears.
A drop,   a parachute
opens and a sin, delicate and fading,
brightens the day.

E-Mail Polemics

EXCELLENT!! EXCELLENT!! EXCELLENT!!

Well said and well written. Upwards and onwards my fellow humans!

——-Original Message——-
From: nicholas powers
Sent: Friday, January 10, 2003 3:09 PM
To: newyork-list@burningman.com
Subject: RE: [BManNYC] OT: UN Weapons Inspectors Find "No Smoking Gun"

From Mr. Metro,

It's too easy to dismiss the major religions of Christianity and Islam as "outmoded and grotesque superstitions" while leaving intact the superstition that structures our daily lives which is Capitalism itself.

It's too easy for us as children of the Empire to cast Mid-East religious fundamentalism as the only form of extremism worth criticizing; it helps eclipse the fact that we are economic fundamentalists. Why so? Because at the recent Winter Decompression there was a lounge staffed by a woman in a French maid outfit reading me and my girlfriend's name off a blank piece of paper, it was her "guest list." Once inside we saw littered all over the floor fake thousand dollar bills and with this fake money you could buy a kiss, a hug or an experience. I slammed a poem for 4 grand, not bad for two minutes worth of work but I think Saul Williams makes more. Anyway, I got the "point" of the art, which was money is a superstition, it only has validity because we believe in it the same way Muslims believe in Islam. We are witnessing a world being rent apart by two competing fanaticisms, not one.

Oil drives our economy, and our economy, dollar bills and all, is only the latest superstition we are addicted to and addiction is the exact term we must use here. We crave Order. The price of being human is being addicted to a system of belief that creates a psychological person, aka a *self*, from the physical drives of the body but once we have a *self* based on some Order of Knowledge, we must keep it stable or lose our hard won *selves* into anxiety. Remember 911, the surreal horror of feeling like the world was going to end. Why? Because the symbols of our Order of Knowledge, the World Trade Center, Pentagon and White House were attacked. Tomorrow is less a time than a place we arrive at again and again, always lost, always looking for directions.

As for the pleasure of McDonalds versus the pain of converting to Islam, well of course to us our system seems benign. If we don't support American Capitalism it falls from the inside out. First, if our superstition is purchased by the world, it will ecologically devastate the planet in a century. Second, the logic of Capitalism is boom and bust. Corporations compete for consumers by offering cheaper goods. Since CEO's aren't lowering their million dollar salaries, that means cheaper and cheaper labor; which means workers can't afford the goods they produce, which becomes a Recession as the markets become glutted with un-buyable stuff. Poverty is a part of Capitalism not its enemy. In fact, if everyone in the world got a living wage Capitalism would be economically impossible, that's why multinationals force "developing countries" to underbid each other, to offer lower wages and fewer environmental rules, hardly productive toward human freedom.

Last two points, human nature is not violent because there is no such thing. We as a species kill in the name of (fill in the blank) because our artificial selves are based on a system of naming and we prefer to kill each other than question the superstition that guarantees our selves. Last point, the choice isn't between a world of benevolent Capitalism or Muslim Fanaticism, to reduce our options to those two is false. It's between the freedom of the human imagination or terror of the Other becoming terrorism itself. All beliefs lose their believers, all things become history, and someday so will history itself because we too will be gone. Neither Islam nor Capitalism will last longer than humanity. Our brothers and sisters in the Mid-East and here in the U.S.

will find something else to believe in. Our future depends on us creating that belief together.

Another world is possible.

UpSet Press, Ink. is a knot for prophets, with 501 followers as tax-evaders, who organize bias in Brooklyn, and hound foster care homes for communists aware that the means of production for visual art is litter that doesn't decompose in polite circles.

It is the oven flame of UpSet Press that provides Last Suppers to incorrigible artists who up-end statues that suggestively alter native viewpoints and privatize public volatility.

Appendix

The National Security Strategy of the United States of America

TABLE OF CONTENTS

Introduction: The White House

The great struggles of the twentieth century between liberty and totalitarianism ended with a decisive victory for the forces of freedom-and a single sustainable model for national success: freedom, democracy, and free enterprise. In the twenty-first century, only nations that share a commitment to protecting basic human rights and guaranteeing political and economic freedom will be able to unleash the potential of their people and assure their future prosperity. People everywhere want to be able to speak freely; choose who will govern them; worship as they please; educate their children-male and female; own property; and enjoy the benefits of their labor. These values of freedom are right and true for every person, in every society-and the duty of protecting these values against their enemies is the common calling of freedom-loving people across the globe and across the ages.

Today, the United States enjoys a position of unparalleled military strength and great economic and political influence. In keeping with our heritage and principles, we do not use our strength to press for unilateral advantage. We seek instead to create a balance of power that favors human freedom: conditions in which all nations and all societies can choose for themselves the rewards and challenges of political and economic liberty. In a world that is safe, people will be able to make their own lives better. We will defend the peace by fighting terrorists and tyrants. We will preserve the peace by building good relations among the great powers. We will extend the peace by encouraging free and open societies on every continent.

Defending our Nation against its enemies is the first and fundamental commitment of the Federal Government. Today, that task has changed dramatically. Enemies in the past needed great armies and great industrial capabilities to endanger America. Now, shadowy networks of individuals can bring great chaos and suffering to our shores for less than it costs to purchase a single tank. Terrorists are organized to penetrate open societies and to turn the power of modern technologies against us.

To defeat this threat we must make use of every tool in our arsenal-military power, better homeland defenses, law enforcement, intelligence, and vigorous efforts to cut off terrorist financing. The war against terrorists of global reach is a global enterprise of uncertain duration. America will help nations that need our assistance in combating terror. And America will hold to account nations that are compromised by terror, including those who harbor terrorists — because the allies of terror are the enemies of civilization. The United States and countries cooperating with us must not allow the terrorists to develop new home bases. Together, we will seek to deny them sanctuary at every turn.

The gravest danger our Nation faces lies at the crossroads of radicalism and technology. Our enemies have openly declared that they are seeking weapons of mass destruction, and evidence indicates that they are doing so with determination. The United States will not allow these efforts to succeed. We will build defenses against ballistic missiles and other means of delivery. We will cooperate with other nations to deny, contain, and curtail our enemies' efforts to acquire dangerous technologies. And, as a matter of common sense and self-defense, America will act against such emerging threats before they are fully formed. We cannot defend America and our friends by hoping for the best. So we must be prepared to defeat our enemies' plans, using the best intelligence and proceeding with deliberation. History will judge harshly those who saw this coming danger but failed to act. In the new world we have entered, the only path to peace and security is the path of action.

As we defend the peace, we will also take advantage of an historic opportunity to preserve the peace. Today, the international community has the best chance since the rise of the nation-state in the seventeenth century to build a world where great powers compete in peace instead of continually prepare for war. Today, the world's great powers find ourselves on the same side — united by common dangers of terrorist violence and chaos. The United States will build on these common interests to promote global security. We are also increasingly united by common values. Russia is in the midst of a hopeful transition, reaching for its democratic future and a partner in the war on terror. Chinese leaders are discovering that economic freedom is the only source of national wealth. In time, they will find that social and political freedom is the only source of national greatness. America will encourage the advancement of democracy and economic openness in both nations, because these are the best foundations for domestic stability and international order. We will strongly resist aggression from other great powers-even as we welcome their peaceful pursuit of prosperity, trade, and cultural advancement.

Finally, the United States will use this moment of opportunity to extend the benefits of freedom across the globe. We will actively work to bring the hope of democracy, development, free markets, and free trade to every corner of the world. The events of September 11, 2001, taught us that weak states, like Afghanistan, can pose as great a danger to our national interests as strong states. Poverty does not make poor people into terrorists and murderers. Yet poverty, weak institutions, and corruption can make weak states vulnerable to terrorist networks and drug cartels within their borders.

The United States will stand beside any nation determined to build a better future by seeking the rewards of liberty for its people. Free trade and free markets have proven their ability to lift whole societies out of poverty-so the United States will work with individual nations, entire regions, and the entire global trading community to build a world that trades in freedom and therefore grows in prosperity. The United States will deliver greater development assistance through the New Millennium Challenge Account to nations that govern justly, invest in their people, and encourage economic freedom. We will also continue to lead the world in efforts to reduce the terrible toll of HIV/AIDS and other infectious diseases.

In building a balance of power that favors freedom, the United States is guided by the conviction that all nations have important responsibilities. Nations that enjoy freedom must actively fight terror. Nations that depend on international stability must help prevent the spread of weapons of mass destruction. Nations that seek international aid must govern themselves wisely, so that aid is well spent. For freedom to thrive, accountability must be expected and required.

We are also guided by the conviction that no nation can build a safer, better world alone. Alliances and multilateral institutions can multiply the strength of freedom-loving nations. The United States is committed to lasting institutions like the United Nations, the World Trade Organization, the Organization of American States, and NATO as well as other long-standing alliances. Coalitions of the willing can augment these permanent institutions. In all cases, international obligations are to be taken seriously. They are not to be undertaken symbolically to rally support for an ideal without furthering its attainment.

Freedom is the non-negotiable demand of human dignity; the birthright of every person-in every civilization. Throughout history, freedom has been threatened by war and terror; it has been challenged by the clashing wills of powerful states and the evil designs of tyrants; and it has been tested by widespread poverty and disease. Today, humanity holds in its hands the opportunity to further freedom's triumph over all these foes. The United States welcomes our responsibility to lead in this great mission.

George W. Bush
THE WHITE HOUSE,
September 17, 2002

Appendix

I. Overview of America's International Strategy

"Our Nation's cause has always been larger than our Nation's defense. We fight, as we always fight, for a just peace-a peace that favors liberty. We will defend the peace against the threats from terrorists and tyrants. We will preserve the peace by building good relations among the great powers. And we will extend the peace by encouraging free and open societies on every continent."

President Bush
West Point, New York
June 1, 2002

The United States possesses unprecedented — and unequaled-strength and influence in the world. Sustained by faith in the principles of liberty, and the value of a free society, this position comes with unparalleled responsibilities, obligations, and opportunity. The great strength of this nation must be used to promote a balance of power that favors freedom.

For most of the twentieth century, the world was divided by a great struggle over ideas: destructive totalitarian visions versus freedom and equality.

That great struggle is over. The militant visions of class, nation, and race, which promised utopia and delivered misery have been defeated and discredited. America is now threatened less by conquering states than we are by failing ones. We are menaced less by fleets and armies than by catastrophic technologies in the hands of the embittered few. We must defeat these threats to our Nation, allies, and friends.

This is also a time of opportunity for America. We will work to translate this moment of influence into decades of peace, prosperity, and liberty. The U.S. national security strategy will be based on a distinctly American internationalism that reflects the union of our values and our national interests. The aim of this strategy is to help make the world not just safer but better. Our goals on the path to progress are clear: political and economic freedom, peaceful relations with other states, and respect for human dignity.

And this path is not America's alone. It is open to all. To achieve these goals, the United States will:

- champion aspirations for human dignity;
- strengthen alliances to defeat global terrorism and work to prevent attacks against us and our friends;
- work with others to defuse regional conflicts;
- prevent our enemies from threatening us, our allies, and our friends, with weapons of mass destruction;
- ignite a new era of global economic growth through free markets and free trade;
- expand the circle of development by opening societies and building the infrastructure of democracy;
- develop agendas for cooperative action with other main centers of global power; and

- transform America's national security institutions to meet the challenges and opportunities of the twenty-first century.

II. Champion Aspirations for Human Dignity

"Some worry that it is somehow undiplomatic or impolite to speak the language of right and wrong. I disagree. Different circumstances require different methods, but not different moralities."

President Bush
West Point, New York
June 1, 2002

In pursuit of our goals, our first imperative is to clarify what we stand for: the United States must defend liberty and justice because these principles are right and true for all people everywhere. No nation owns these aspirations, and no nation is exempt from them. Fathers and mothers in all societies want their children to be educated and to live free from poverty and violence. No people on earth yearn to be oppressed, aspire to servitude, or eagerly await the midnight knock of the secret police.

America must stand firmly for the nonnegotiable demands of human dignity: the rule of law; limits on the absolute power of the state; free speech; freedom of worship; equal justice; respect for women; religious and ethnic tolerance; and respect for private property.

These demands can be met in many ways. America's constitution has served us well. Many other nations, with different histories and cultures, facing different circumstances, have successfully incorporated these core principles into their own systems of governance. History has not been kind to those nations that ignored or flouted the rights and aspirations of their people.

America's experience as a great multi-ethnic democracy affirms our conviction that people of many heritages and faiths can live and prosper in peace. Our own history is a long struggle to live up to our ideals. But even in our worst moments, the principles enshrined in the Declaration of Independence were there to guide us. As a result, America is not just a stronger, but is a freer and more just society.

Today, these ideals are a lifeline to lonely defenders of liberty. And when openings arrive, we can encourage change-as we did in central and eastern Europe between 1989 and 1991, or in Belgrade in 2000.When we see democratic processes take hold among our friends in Taiwan or in the Republic of Korea, and see elected leaders replace generals in Latin America and Africa, we see examples of how authoritarian systems can evolve, marrying local history and traditions with the principles we all cherish.

Embodying lessons from our past and using the opportunity we have today, the national security strategy of the United States must start from these core beliefs and look outward for possibilities to expand liberty.

Our principles will guide our government's decisions about international cooperation, the character of our foreign assistance, and the allocation of resources. They will guide our actions and our words in international bodies.

We will:

- speak out honestly about violations of the nonnegotiable demands of human dignity using our voice and vote in international institutions to advance freedom;
- use our foreign aid to promote freedom and support those who struggle non-violently for it, ensuring that nations moving toward democracy are rewarded for the steps they take;
- make freedom and the development of democratic institutions key themes in our bilateral relations, seeking solidarity and cooperation from other democracies while we press governments that deny human rights to move toward a better future; and
- take special efforts to promote freedom of religion and conscience and defend it from encroachment by repressive governments.

We will champion the cause of human dignity and oppose those who resist it.

III. Strengthen Alliances to Defeat Global Terrorism and Work to Prevent Attacks Against Us and Our Friends

"Just three days removed from these events, Americans do not yet have the distance of history. But our responsibility to history is already clear: to answer these attacks and rid the world of evil. War has been waged against us by stealth and deceit and murder. This nation is peaceful, but fierce when stirred to anger. The conflict was begun on the timing and terms of others. It will end in a way, and at an hour, of our choosing."

President Bush
Washington, D.C. (The National Cathedral)
September 14, 2001

The United States of America is fighting a war against terrorists of global reach. The enemy is not a single political regime or person or religion or ideology. The enemy is terrorism — premeditated, politically motivated violence perpetrated against innocents.

In many regions, legitimate grievances prevent the emergence of a lasting peace. Such grievances deserve to be, and must be, addressed within a political process. But no cause justifies terror. The United States will make no concessions to terrorist demands and strike no deals with them. We make no distinction between terrorists and those who knowingly harbor or provide aid to them.

The struggle against global terrorism is different from any other war in our history. It will be fought on many fronts against a particularly elusive enemy over an extended period of time. Progress will come through the persistent accumulation of successes-some seen, some unseen.

Today our enemies have seen the results of what civilized nations can, and will, do against regimes that harbor, support, and use terrorism to achieve their political goals. Afghanistan has been liberated; coalition forces continue to hunt down the Taliban and al-Qaida. But it is not only this battlefield on which we will engage terrorists. Thousands of trained terrorists remain at large with cells in North America, South America, Europe, Africa, the Middle East, and across Asia.

Our priority will be first to disrupt and destroy terrorist organizations of global reach and attack their leadership; command, control, and communications; material support; and finances. This will have a disabling effect upon the terrorists' ability to plan and operate.

We will continue to encourage our regional partners to take up a coordinated effort that isolates the terrorists. Once the regional campaign localizes the threat to a particular state, we will help ensure the state has the military, law enforcement, political, and financial tools necessary to finish the task.

The United States will continue to work with our allies to disrupt the financing of terrorism. We will identify and block the sources of funding for terrorism, freeze the assets of terrorists and those who support them, deny terrorists access to the international financial system, protect legitimate charities from being abused by terrorists, and prevent the movement of terrorists' assets through alternative financial networks.

However, this campaign need not be sequential to be effective, the cumulative effect across all regions will help achieve the results we seek. We will disrupt and destroy terrorist organizations by:

- direct and continuous action using all the elements of national and international power. Our immediate focus will be those terrorist organizations of global reach and any terrorist or state sponsor of terrorism which attempts to gain or use weapons of mass destruction (WMD) or their precursors;
- defending the United States, the American people, and our interests at home and abroad by identifying and destroying the threat before it reaches our borders.While the United States will constantly strive to enlist the support of the international community, we will not hesitate to act alone, if necessary, to exercise our right of selfdefense by acting preemptively against such terrorists, to prevent them from doing harm against our people and our country; and
- denying further sponsorship, support, and sanctuary to terrorists by convincing or compelling states to accept their sovereign responsibilities. We will also wage a war of ideas to win the battle against international terrorism. This includes:
- using the full influence of the United States, and working closely with allies and friends, to make clear that all acts of terrorism are illegitimate so that terrorism will be viewed in the same light as slavery, piracy, or genocide: behavior that no respectable government can condone or support and all must oppose;
- supporting moderate and modern government, especially in the Muslim world, to ensure that the conditions and ideologies that promote terrorism do not find fertile ground in any nation;
- diminishing the underlying conditions that spawn terrorism by enlisting the international community to focus its efforts and resources on areas most at risk; and
- using effective public diplomacy to promote the free flow of information and ideas to kindle the hopes and aspirations of freedom of those in societies ruled by the sponsors of global terrorism.

While we recognize that our best defense is a good offense, we are also strengthening America's homeland security to protect against and deter attack. This Administration has proposed the largest government reorganization since the Truman Administration created the National Security Council and the Department of Defense. Centered on a new Department of Homeland Security and including a new unified military command and a fundamental reordering of the FBI, our comprehensive plan to secure the homeland encompasses every level of government and the cooperation of the public and the private sector.

This strategy will turn adversity into opportunity. For example, emergency management systems will be better able to cope not just with terrorism but with all hazards. Our medical system will be strengthened to manage not just bioterror, but all infectious diseases and mass-casualty dangers. Our border controls will not just stop terrorists, but improve the efficient movement of legitimate traffic.

While our focus is protecting America, we know that to defeat terrorism in today's globalized world we need support from our allies and friends. Wherever possible, the United States will rely on regional organizations and state powers to meet their obligations to fight terrorism. Where governments find the fight against terrorism beyond their capacities, we will match their willpower and their resources with whatever help we and our allies can provide.

As we pursue the terrorists in Afghanistan, we will continue to work with international organizations such as the United Nations, as well as non-governmental organizations, and other countries to provide the humanitarian, political, economic, and security assistance necessary to rebuild Afghanistan so that it will never again abuse its people, threaten its neighbors, and provide a haven for terrorists.

In the war against global terrorism, we will never forget that we are ultimately fighting for our democratic values and way of life. Freedom and fear are at war, and there will be no quick or easy end to this conflict. In leading the campaign against terrorism, we are forging new, productive international relationships and redefining existing ones in ways that meet the challenges of the twenty-first century.

IV. Work with others to Defuse Regional Conflicts

"We build a world of justice, or we will live in a world of coercion. The magnitude of our shared responsibilities makes our disagreements look so small."

President Bush
Berlin, Germany
May 23, 2002

Concerned nations must remain actively engaged in critical regional disputes to avoid explosive escalation and minimize human suffering. In an increasingly interconnected world, regional crisis can strain our alliances, rekindle rivalries among the major powers, and create horrifying affronts to human dignity. When violence erupts and states falter, the United States will work with friends and partners to alleviate suffering and restore stability.

No doctrine can anticipate every circumstance in which U.S. action-direct or indirect-is warranted. We have finite political, economic, and military resources to meet our global priorities. The United States will approach each case with these strategic principles in mind:

- The United States should invest time and resources into building international relationships and institutions that can help manage local crises when they emerge.
- The United States should be realistic about its ability to help those who are unwilling or unready to help themselves. Where and when people are ready to do their part, we will be willing to move decisively.

The Israeli-Palestinian conflict is critical because of the toll of human suffering, because of America's close relationship with the state of Israel and key Arab states, and because of that region's importance to other global priorities of the United States. There can be no peace for either side without freedom for both sides. America stands committed to an independent and democratic Palestine, living beside Israel in peace and security. Like all other people, Palestinians deserve a government that serves their interests and listens to their voices. The United States will continue to encourage all parties to step up to their responsibilities as we seek a just and comprehensive settlement to the conflict.

The United States, the international donor community, and the World Bank stand ready to work with a reformed Palestinian government on economic development, increased humanitarian assistance, and a program to establish, finance, and monitor a truly independent judiciary. If Palestinians embrace democracy, and the rule of law, confront corruption, and firmly reject terror, they can count on American support for the creation of a Palestinian state.

Israel also has a large stake in the success of a democratic Palestine. Permanent occupation threatens Israel's identity and democracy. So the United States continues to challenge Israeli leaders to take concrete steps to support the emergence of a viable, credible Palestinian state. As there is progress towards security, Israel forces need to withdraw fully to positions they held prior to September 28, 2000. And consistent with the recommendations of the Mitchell Committee, Israeli settlement activity in the occupied territories must stop. As violence subsides, freedom of movement should be restored, permitting innocent Palestinians to resume work and normal life. The United States can play a crucial role but, ultimately, lasting peace can only come when Israelis and Palestinians resolve the issues and end the conflict between them.

In South Asia, the United States has also emphasized the need for India and Pakistan to resolve their disputes. This Administration invested time and resources building strong bilateral relations with India and Pakistan. These strong relations then gave us leverage to play a constructive role when tensions in the region became acute. With Pakistan, our bilateral relations have been bolstered by Pakistan's choice to join the war against terror and move toward building a more open and tolerant society. The Administration sees India's potential to become one of the great democratic powers of the twenty first century and has worked hard to transform our relationship accordingly. Our involvement in this regional dispute, building on earlier investments in bilateral relations, looks first to concrete steps by India and Pakistan that can help defuse military confrontation.

Indonesia took courageous steps to create a working democracy and respect for the rule of law. By tolerating ethnic minorities, respecting the rule of law, and accepting open markets, Indonesia may be able to employ the engine of opportunity that has helped lift some of its neighbors out of poverty and desperation. It is the initiative by Indonesia that allows U.S. assistance to make a difference.

In the Western Hemisphere we have formed flexible coalitions with countries that share our priorities, particularly Mexico, Brazil, Canada, Chile, and Colombia. Together we will promote a truly democratic hemisphere where our integration advances security, prosperity, opportunity, and hope. We will work with regional institutions, such as the Summit of the Americas process, the Organization of American States (OAS), and the Defense Ministerial of the Americas for the benefit of the entire hemisphere.

Parts of Latin America confront regional conflict, especially arising from the violence of drug cartels and their accomplices. This conflict and unrestrained narcotics trafficking could imperil the health and security of the United States. Therefore we have developed an active strategy to help the Andean nations adjust their economies, enforce their laws, defeat terrorist organizations, and cut off the supply of drugs, while-as important-we work to reduce the demand for drugs in our own country.

In Colombia, we recognize the link between terrorist and extremist groups that challenge the security of the state and drug trafficking activities that help finance the operations of such groups. We are working to help Colombia defend its democratic institutions and defeat illegal armed groups of both the left and right by extending effective sovereignty over the entire national territory and provide basic security to the Colombian people.

In Africa, promise and opportunity sit side by side with disease, war, and desperate poverty. This threatens both a core value of the United States — preserving human dignity-and our strategic priority-combating global terror. American interests and American principles, therefore, lead in the same direction: we will work with others for an African continent that lives in liberty, peace, and growing prosperity. Together with our European allies, we must help strengthen Africa's fragile states, help build indigenous capability to secure porous borders, and help build up the law enforcement and intelligence infrastructure to deny havens for terrorists.

An ever more lethal environment exists in Africa as local civil wars spread beyond borders to create regional war zones. Forming coalitions of the willing and cooperative security arrangements are key to confronting these emerging transnational threats.

Africa's great size and diversity requires a security strategy that focuses on bilateral engagement and builds coalitions of the willing. This Administration will focus on three interlocking strategies for the region:

- countries with major impact on their neighborhood such as South Africa, Nigeria, Kenya, and Ethiopia are anchors for regional engagement and require focused attention;
- coordination with European allies and international institutions is essential for constructive conflict mediation and successful peace operations; and
- Africa's capable reforming states and sub-regional organizations must be strengthened as the primary means to address transnational threats on a sustained basis.

Ultimately the path of political and economic freedom presents the surest route to progress in sub-Saharan Africa, where most wars are conflicts over material resources and political access often tragically waged on the basis of ethnic and religious difference. The transition to the African Union with its stated commitment to good governance and a common responsibility for democratic political systems offers opportunities to strengthen democracy on the continent.

V. Prevent Our Enemies from Threatening Us, Our Allies, and Our Friends with Weapons of Mass Destruction

"The gravest danger to freedom lies at the crossroads of radicalism and technology. When the spread of chemical and biological and nuclear weapons, along with ballistic missile technology-when that occurs, even weak states and small groups could attain a catastrophic power to strike great nations. Our enemies have declared this very intention, and have been caught seeking these terrible weapons. They want the capability to blackmail us, or to harm us, or to harm our friends-and we will oppose them with all our power."

President Bush
West Point, New York
June 1, 2002

The nature of the Cold War threat required the United States-with our allies and friends-to emphasize deterrence of the enemy's use of force, producing a grim strategy of mutual assured destruction. With the collapse of the Soviet Union and the end of the Cold War, our security environment has undergone profound transformation.

Having moved from confrontation to cooperation as the hallmark of our relationship with Russia, the dividends are evident: an end to the balance of terror that divided us; an historic reduction in the nuclear arsenals on both sides; and cooperation in areas such as counter-terrorism and missile defense that until recently were inconceivable.

But new deadly challenges have emerged from rogue states and terrorists. None of these contemporary threats rival the sheer destructive power that was arrayed against us by the Soviet Union. However, the nature and motivations of these new adversaries, their determination to obtain destructive powers hitherto available only to the world's strongest states, and the greater likelihood that they will use weapons of mass destruction against us, make today's security environment more complex and dangerous.

In the 1990s we witnessed the emergence of a small number of rogue states that, while different in important ways, share a number of attributes. These states:

- brutalize their own people and squander their national resources for the personal gain of the rulers;
- display no regard for international law, threaten their neighbors, and callously violate international treaties to which they are party;
- are determined to acquire weapons of mass destruction, along with other advanced military technology, to be used as threats or offensively to achieve the aggressive designs of these regimes;
- sponsor terrorism around the globe; and
- reject basic human values and hate the United States and everything for which it stands.

At the time of the Gulf War, we acquired irrefutable proof that Iraq's designs were not limited to the chemical weapons it had used against Iran and its own people, but also extended to the acquisition of nuclear weapons and biological agents. In the past decade North Korea has become the world's principal purveyor of ballistic missiles, and has tested increasingly capable missiles while developing its own WMD arsenal. Other rogue regimes seek nuclear, biological, and chemical weapons as well. These states' pursuit of, and global trade in, such weapons has become a looming threat to all nations.

We must be prepared to stop rogue states and their terrorist clients before they are able to threaten or use weapons of mass destruction against the United States and our allies and friends. Our response must take full advantage of strengthened alliances, the establishment of new partnerships with former adversaries, innovation in the use of military forces, modern technologies, including the development of an effective missile defense system, and increased emphasis on intelligence collection and analysis.

Our comprehensive strategy to combat WMD includes:

- *Proactive counter-proliferation efforts.* We must deter and defend against the threat before it is unleashed. We must ensure that key capabilities-detection, active and passive defenses, and counterforce capabilities-are integrated into our defense transformation and our homeland security systems. Counter-proliferation must also be integrated into the doctrine, training, and equipping of our forces and those of our allies to ensure that we can prevail in any conflict with WMD-armed adversaries.
- *Strengthened nonproliferation efforts to prevent rogue states and terrorists from acquiring the materials, technologies, and expertise necessary for weapons of mass destruction.* We will enhance diplomacy, arms control, multilateral export controls, and threat reduction assistance that impede states and terrorists seeking WMD, and when necessary, interdict enabling technologies and materials. We will continue to build coalitions to support these efforts, encouraging their increased political and financial support for nonproliferation and threat reduction programs. The recent G-8 agreement to commit up to $20 billion to a global partnership against proliferation marks a major step forward.
- *Effective consequence management to respond to the effects of WMD use, whether by terrorists or hostile states.* Minimizing the effects of WMD use against our people will help deter those who possess such weapons and dissuade those who seek to acquire them by persuading enemies that they cannot attain their desired ends. The United States must also be prepared to respond to the effects of WMD use against our forces abroad, and to help friends and allies if they are attacked.

It has taken almost a decade for us to comprehend the true nature of this new threat. Given the goals of rogue states and terrorists, the United States can no longer solely rely on a reactive posture as we have in the past. The inability to deter a potential attacker, the immediacy of today's threats, and the magnitude of potential harm that could be caused by our adversaries' choice of weapons, do not permit that option. We cannot let our enemies strike first.

In the Cold War, especially following the Cuban missile crisis, we faced a generally status quo, risk-averse adversary. Deterrence was an effective defense. But deterrence based only upon the threat of retaliation is less likely to work against leaders of rogue states more willing to take risks, gambling with the lives of their people, and the wealth of their nations.

- In the Cold War, weapons of mass destruction were considered weapons of last resort whose use risked the destruction of those who used them. Today, our enemies see weapons of mass destruction as weapons of choice. For rogue states these weapons are tools of intimidation and military aggression against their neighbors. These weapons may also allow these states to attempt to blackmail the United States and our allies to prevent us from deterring or repelling the aggressive behavior of rogue states. Such states also see these weapons as their best means of overcoming the conventional superiority of the United States.
- Traditional concepts of deterrence will not work against a terrorist enemy whose avowed tactics are wanton destruction and the targeting of innocents; whose so-called soldiers seek martyrdom in death and whose most potent protection is statelessness. The overlap between states that sponsor terror and those that pursue WMD compels us to action.

For centuries, international law recognized that nations need not suffer an attack before they can lawfully take action to defend themselves against forces that present an imminent danger of attack. Legal scholars and international jurists often conditioned the legitimacy of preemption on the existence of an imminent threat-most often a visible mobilization of armies, navies, and air forces preparing to attack.

We must adapt the concept of imminent threat to the capabilities and objectives of today's adversaries. Rogue states and terrorists do not seek to attack us using conventional means. They know such attacks would fail. Instead, they rely on acts of terror and, potentially, the use of weapons of mass destruction-weapons that can be easily concealed, delivered covertly, and used without warning.

The targets of these attacks are our military forces and our civilian population, in direct violation of one of the principal norms of the law of warfare. As was demonstrated by the losses on September 11, 2001, mass civilian casualties is the specific objective of terrorists and these losses would be exponentially more severe if terrorists acquired and used weapons of mass destruction.

The United States has long maintained the option of preemptive actions to counter a sufficient threat to our national security. The greater the threat, the greater is the risk of inaction — and the more compelling the case for taking anticipatory action to defend ourselves, even if uncertainty remains as to the time and place of the enemy's attack. To forestall or prevent such hostile acts by our adversaries, the United States will, if necessary, act preemptively.

The United States will not use force in all cases to preempt emerging threats, nor should nations use preemption as a pretext for aggression. Yet in an age where the enemies of civilization openly and actively seek the world's most destructive technologies, the United States cannot remain idle while dangers gather. We will always proceed deliberately, weighing the consequences of our actions. To support preemptive options, we will:

- build better, more integrated intelligence capabilities to provide timely, accurate information on threats, wherever they may emerge;
- coordinate closely with allies to form a common assessment of the most dangerous threats; and
- continue to transform our military forces to ensure our ability to conduct rapid and precise operations to achieve decisive results.

The purpose of our actions will always be to eliminate a specific threat to the United States or our allies and friends. The reasons for our actions will be clear, the force measured, and the cause just.

VI. Ignite a New Era of Global Economic Growth through Free Markets and Free Trade

"When nations close their markets and opportunity is hoarded by a privileged few, no amount-no amount-of development aid is ever enough. When nations respect their people, open markets, invest in better health and education, every dollar of aid, every dollar of trade revenue and domestic capital is used more effectively."

President Bush
Monterrey, Mexico
March 22, 2002

A strong world economy enhances our national security by advancing prosperity and freedom in the rest of the world. Economic growth supported by free trade and free markets creates new jobs and higher incomes. It allows people to lift their lives out of poverty, spurs economic and legal reform, and the fight against corruption, and it reinforces the habits of liberty.

We will promote economic growth and economic freedom beyond America's shores. All governments are responsible for creating their own economic policies and responding to their own economic challenges. We will use our economic engagement with other countries to underscore the benefits of policies that generate higher productivity and sustained economic growth, including:

- pro-growth legal and regulatory policies to encourage business investment, innovation, and entrepreneurial activity;
- tax policies-particularly lower marginal tax rates-that improve incentives for work and investment;
- rule of law and intolerance of corruption so that people are confident that they will be able to enjoy the fruits of their economic endeavors;
- strong financial systems that allow capital to be put to its most efficient use;
- sound fiscal policies to support business activity;
- investments in health and education that improve the well-being and skills of the labor force and population as a whole; and
- free trade that provides new avenues for growth and fosters the diffusion of technologies and ideas that increase productivity and opportunity.

The lessons of history are clear: market economies, not command-and-control economies with the heavy hand of government, are the best way to promote prosperity and reduce poverty. Policies that further strengthen market incentives and market institutions are relevant for all economies-industrialized countries, emerging markets, and the developing world.

A return to strong economic growth in Europe and Japan is vital to U.S. national security interests. We want our allies to have strong economies for their own sake, for the sake of the global economy, and for the sake of global security. European efforts to remove structural barriers in their economies are particularly important in this regard, as are Japan's efforts to end deflation and address the problems of non-performing loans in the Japanese banking system. We will continue to use our regular consultations with Japan and our European partners-including through the Group of Seven (G-7)-to discuss policies they are adopting to promote growth in their economies and support higher global economic growth.

Improving stability in emerging markets is also key to global economic growth. International flows of investment capital are needed to expand the productive potential of these economies. These flows allow emerging markets and developing countries to make the investments that raise living standards and reduce poverty. Our long-term objective should be a world in which all countries have investment-grade credit ratings that allow them access to international capital markets and to invest in their future.

We are committed to policies that will help emerging markets achieve access to larger capital flows at lower cost. To this end, we will continue to pursue reforms aimed at reducing uncertainty in financial markets. We will work actively with other countries, the International Monetary Fund (IMF), and the private sector to implement the G-7 Action Plan negotiated earlier this year for preventing financial crises and more effectively resolving them when they occur.

The best way to deal with financial crises is to prevent them from occurring, and we have encouraged the IMF to improve its efforts doing so. We will continue to work with the IMF to streamline the policy conditions for its lending and to focus its lending strategy on achieving economic growth through sound fiscal and monetary policy, exchange rate policy, and financial sector policy.

The concept of "free trade" arose as a moral principle even before it became a pillar of economics. If you can make something that others value, you should be able to sell it to them. If others make something that you value, you should be able to buy it. This is real freedom, the freedom for a person-or a nation-to make a living. To promote free trade, the Unites States has developed a comprehensive strategy:

- *Seize the global initiative.* The new global trade negotiations we helped launch at Doha in November 2001 will have an ambitious agenda, especially in agriculture, manufacturing, and services, targeted for completion in 2005. The United States has led the way in completing the accession of China and a democratic Taiwan to the World Trade Organization. We will assist Russia's preparations to join the WTO.
- *Press regional initiatives.* The United States and other democracies in the Western Hemisphere have agreed to create the Free Trade Area of the Americas, targeted for completion in 2005. This year the United States will advocate market-access negotiations with its partners, targeted on agriculture, industrial goods, services, investment, and government procurement. We will also offer more opportunity to the poorest continent, Africa, starting with full use of the preferences allowed in the African Growth and Opportunity Act, and leading to free trade.

- *Move ahead with bilateral free trade agreements.* Building on the free trade agreement with Jordan enacted in 2001, the Administration will work this year to complete free trade agreements with Chile and Singapore. Our aim is to achieve free trade agreements with a mix of developed and developing countries in all regions of the world. Initially, Central America, Southern Africa, Morocco, and Australia will be our principal focal points.
- *Renew the executive-congressional partnership.* Every administration's trade strategy depends on a productive partnership with Congress. After a gap of 8 years, the Administration reestablished majority support in the Congress for trade liberalization by passing Trade Promotion Authority and the other market opening measures for developing countries in the Trade Act of 2002. This Administration will work with Congress to enact new bilateral, regional, and global trade agreements that will be concluded under the recently passed Trade Promotion Authority.
- *Promote the connection between trade and development.* Trade policies can help developing countries strengthen property rights, competition, the rule of law, investment, the spread of knowledge, open societies, the efficient allocation of resources, and regional integration-all leading to growth, opportunity, and confidence in developing countries. The United States is implementing The Africa Growth and Opportunity Act to provide market-access for nearly all goods produced in the 35 countries of sub — Saharan Africa. We will make more use of this act and its equivalent for the Caribbean Basin and continue to work with multilateral and regional institutions to help poorer countries take advantage of these opportunities. Beyond market access, the most important area where trade intersects with poverty is in public health. We will ensure that the WTO intellectual property rules are flexible enough to allow developing nations to gain access to critical medicines for extraordinary dangers like HIV/AIDS, tuberculosis, and malaria.
- *Enforce trade agreements and laws against unfair practices.* Commerce depends on the rule of law; international trade depends on enforceable agreements. Our top priorities are to resolve ongoing disputes with the European Union, Canada, and Mexico and to make a global effort to address new technology, science, and health regulations that needlessly impede farm exports and improved agriculture. Laws against unfair trade practices are often abused, but the international community must be able to address genuine concerns about government subsidies and dumping. International industrial espionage, which undermines fair competition, must be detected and deterred.
- *Help domestic industries and workers adjust.* There is a sound statutory framework for these transitional safeguards which we have used in the agricultural sector and which we are using this year to help the American steel industry. The benefits of free trade depend upon the enforcement of fair trading practices. These safeguards help ensure that the benefits of free trade do not come at the expense of American workers. Trade adjustment assistance will help workers adapt to the change and dynamism of open markets.

- *Protect the environment and workers.* The United States must foster economic growth in ways that will provide a better life along with widening prosperity. We will incorporate labor and environmental concerns into U.S. trade negotiations, creating a healthy "network" between multilateral environmental agreements with the WTO, and use the International Labor Organization, trade preference programs, and trade talks to improve working conditions in conjunction with freer trade.
- *Enhance energy security.* We will strengthen our own energy security and the shared prosperity of the global economy by working with our allies, trading partners, and energy producers to expand the sources and types of global energy supplied, especially in the Western Hemisphere, Africa, Central Asia, and the Caspian region. We will also continue to work with our partners to develop cleaner and more energy efficient technologies.

Economic growth should be accompanied by global efforts to stabilize greenhouse gas concentrations associated with this growth, containing them at a level that prevents dangerous human interference with the global climate. Our overall objective is to reduce America's greenhouse gas emissions relative to the size of our economy, cutting such emissions per unit of economic activity by 18 percent over the next 10 years, by the year 2012. Our strategies for attaining this goal will be to:

- remain committed to the basic U.N. Framework Convention for international cooperation;
- obtain agreements with key industries to cut emissions of some of the most potent greenhouse gases and give transferable credits to companies that can show real cuts;
- develop improved standards for measuring and registering emission reductions;
- promote renewable energy production and clean coal technology, as well as nuclear power-which produces no greenhouse gas emissions, while also improving fuel economy for U.S. cars and trucks;
- increase spending on research and new conservation technologies, to a total of $4.5 billion-the largest sum being spent on climate change by any country in the world and a $700 million increase over last year's budget; and
- assist developing countries, especially the major greenhouse gas emitters such as China and India, so that they will have the tools and resources to join this effort and be able to grow along a cleaner and better path.

VII. Expand the Circle of Development by Opening Societies and Building the Infrastructure of Democracy

"In World War II we fought to make the world safer, then worked to rebuild it. As we wage war today to keep the world safe from terror, we must also work to make the world a better place for all its citizens."

President Bush
Washington, D.C. (Inter-American Development Bank)
March 14, 2002

A world where some live in comfort and plenty, while half of the human race lives on less than $2 a day, is neither just nor stable. Including all of the world's poor in an expanding circle of development-and opportunity-is a moral imperative and one of the top priorities of U.S. international policy.

Decades of massive development assistance have failed to spur economic growth in the poorest countries. Worse, development aid has often served to prop up failed policies, relieving the pressure for reform and perpetuating misery. Results of aid are typically measured in dollars spent by donors, not in the rates of growth and poverty reduction achieved by recipients. These are the indicators of a failed strategy.

Working with other nations, the United States is confronting this failure. We forged a new consensus at the U.N. Conference on Financing for Development in Monterrey that the objectives of assistance-and the strategies to achieve those objectives-must change.

This Administration's goal is to help unleash the productive potential of individuals in all nations. Sustained growth and poverty reduction is impossible without the right national policies. Where governments have implemented real policy changes, we will provide significant new levels of assistance. The United States and other developed countries should set an ambitious and specific target: to double the size of the world's poorest economies within a decade.

The United States Government will pursue these major strategies to achieve this goal:

- *Provide resources to aid countries that have met the challenge of national reform.* We propose a 50 percent increase in the core development assistance given by the United States. While continuing our present programs, including humanitarian assistance based on need alone, these billions of new dollars will form a new Millennium Challenge Account for projects in countries whose governments rule justly, invest in their people, and encourage economic freedom. Governments must fight corruption, respect basic human rights, embrace the rule of law, invest in health care and education, follow responsible economic policies, and enable entrepreneurship. The Millennium Challenge Account will reward countries that have demonstrated real policy change and challenge those that have not to implement reforms.

- *Improve the effectiveness of the World Bank and other development banks in raising living standards.* The United States is committed to a comprehensive reform agenda for making the World Bank and the other multilateral development banks more effective in improving the lives of the world's poor. We have reversed the downward trend in U.S. contributions and proposed an 18 percent increase in the U.S. contributions to the International Development Association (IDA)-the World Bank's fund for the poorest countries-and the African Development Fund. The key to raising living standards and reducing poverty around the world is increasing productivity growth, especially in the poorest countries. We will continue to press the multilateral development banks to focus on activities that increase economic productivity, such as improvements in education, health, rule of law, and private sector development. Every project, every loan, every grant must be judged by how much it will increase productivity growth in developing countries.
- *Insist upon measurable results to ensure that development assistance is actually making a difference in the lives of the world's poor.* When it comes to economic development, what really matters is that more children are getting a better education, more people have access to health care and clean water, or more workers can find jobs to make a better future for their families. We have a moral obligation to measure the success of our development assistance by whether it is delivering results. For this reason, we will continue to demand that our own development assistance as well as assistance from the multilateral development banks has measurable goals and concrete benchmarks for achieving those goals. Thanks to U.S. leadership, the recent IDA replenishment agreement will establish a monitoring and evaluation system that measures recipient countries' progress. For the first time, donors can link a portion of their contributions to IDA to the achievement of actual development results, and part of the U.S. contribution is linked in this way. We will strive to make sure that the World Bank and other multilateral development banks build on this progress so that a focus on results is an integral part of everything that these institutions do.
- *Increase the amount of development assistance that is provided in the form of grants instead of loans.* Greater use of results-based grants is the best way to help poor countries make productive investments, particularly in the social sectors, without saddling them with ever-larger debt burdens. As a result of U.S. leadership, the recent IDA agreement provided for significant increases in grant funding for the poorest countries for education, HIV/AIDS, health, nutrition, water, sanitation, and other human needs. Our goal is to build on that progress by increasing the use of grants at the other multilateral development banks. We will also challenge universities, nonprofits, and the private sector to match government efforts by using grants to support development projects that show results.
- *Open societies to commerce and investment. Trade and investment are the real engines of economic growth.* Even if government aid increases, most money

for development must come from trade, domestic capital, and foreign investment. An effective strategy must try to expand these flows as well. Free markets and free trade are key priorities of our national security strategy.

- *Secure public health.* The scale of the public health crisis in poor countries is enormous. In countries afflicted by epidemics and pandemics like HIV/AIDS, malaria, and tuberculosis, growth and development will be threatened until these scourges can be contained. Resources from the developed world are necessary but will be effective only with honest governance, which supports prevention programs and provides effective local infrastructure. The United States has strongly backed the new global fund for HIV/AIDS organized by U.N. Secretary General Kofi Annan and its focus on combining prevention with a broad strategy for treatment and care. The United States already contributes more than twice as much money to such efforts as the next largest donor. If the global fund demonstrates its promise, we will be ready to give even more.
- *Emphasize education.* Literacy and learning are the foundation of democracy and development. Only about 7 percent of World Bank resources are devoted to education. This proportion should grow. The United States will increase its own funding for education assistance by at least 20 percent with an emphasis on improving basic education and teacher training in Africa. The United States can also bring information technology to these societies, many of whose education systems have been devastated by HIV/AIDS.
- *Continue to aid agricultural development.* New technologies, including biotechnology, have enormous potential to improve crop yields in developing countries while using fewer pesticides and less water. Using sound science, the United States should help bring these benefits to the 800 million people, including 300 million children, who still suffer from hunger and malnutrition.

VIII. Develop Agendas for Cooperative Action with the Other Main Centers of Global Power

"We have our best chance since the rise of the nation-state in the 17th century to build a world where the great powers compete in peace instead of prepare for war."

President Bush
West Point, New York
June 1, 2002

America will implement its strategies by organizing coalitions-as broad as practicable — of states able and willing to promote a balance of power that favors freedom. Effective coalition leadership requires clear priorities, an appreciation of others' interests, and consistent consultations among partners with a spirit of humility.

There is little of lasting consequence that the United States can accomplish in the world without the sustained cooperation of its allies and friends in Canada and Europe. Europe is also the seat of two of the strongest and most able international institutions in the world: the North Atlantic Treaty Organization (NATO), which has, since its inception, been the fulcrum of transatlantic and inter-European security, and the European Union (EU), our partner in opening world trade.

The attacks of September 11 were also an attack on NATO, as NATO itself recognized when it invoked its Article V self-defense clause for the first time. NATO's core mission-collective defense of the transatlantic alliance of democracies — remains, but NATO must develop new structures and capabilities to carry out that mission under new circumstances. NATO must build a capability to field, at short notice, highly mobile, specially trained forces whenever they are needed to respond to a threat against any member of the alliance.

The alliance must be able to act wherever our interests are threatened, creating coalitions under NATO's own mandate, as well as contributing to mission-based coalitions. To achieve this, we must:

- expand NATO's membership to those democratic nations willing and able to share the burden of defending and advancing our common interests;
- ensure that the military forces of NATO nations have appropriate combat contributions to make in coalition warfare;
- develop planning processes to enable those contributions to become effective multinational fighting forces;
- take advantage of the technological opportunities and economies of scale in our defense spending to transform NATO military forces so that they dominate potential aggressors and diminish our vulnerabilities;
- streamline and increase the flexibility of command structures to meet new operational demands and the associated requirements of training,

integrating, and experimenting with new force configurations; and
- maintain the ability to work and fight together as allies even as we take the necessary steps to transform and modernize our forces.

If NATO succeeds in enacting these changes, the rewards will be a partnership as central to the security and interests of its member states as was the case during the Cold War. We will sustain a common perspective on the threats to our societies and improve our ability to take common action in defense of our nations and their interests. At the same time, we welcome our European allies' efforts to forge a greater foreign policy and defense identity with the EU, and commit ourselves to close consultations to ensure that these developments work with NATO. We cannot afford to lose this opportunity to better prepare the family of transatlantic democracies for the challenges to come.

The attacks of September 11 energized America's Asian alliances. Australia invoked the ANZUS Treaty to declare the September 11 was an attack on Australia itself, following that historic decision with the dispatch of some of the world's finest combat forces for Operation Enduring Freedom. Japan and the Republic of Korea provided unprecedented levels of military logistical support within weeks of the terrorist attack. We have deepened cooperation on counter-terrorism with our alliance partners in Thailand and the Philippines and received invaluable assistance from close friends like Singapore and New Zealand.

The war against terrorism has proven that America's alliances in Asia not only underpin regional peace and stability, but are flexible and ready to deal with new challenges. To enhance our Asian alliances and friendships, we will:

- look to Japan to continue forging a leading role in regional and global affairs based on our common interests, our common values, and our close defense and diplomatic cooperation;
- work with South Korea to maintain vigilance towards the North while preparing our alliance to make contributions to the broader stability of the region over the longer term;
- working together to resolve regional and global problems-as we have so many times from the Battle of the Coral Sea to Tora Bora;
- maintain forces in the region that reflect our commitments to our allies, our requirements, our technological advances, and the strategic environment; and
- build on stability provided by these alliances, as well as with institutions such as ASEAN and the Asia-Pacific Economic Cooperation forum, to develop a mix of regional and bilateral strategies to manage change in this dynamic region.

We are attentive to the possible renewal of old patterns of great power competition. Several potential great powers are now in the midst of internal transition-most importantly Russia, India, and China. In all three cases, recent developments have encouraged our hope that a truly global consensus about basic principles is slowly taking shape.

With Russia, we are already building a new strategic relationship based on a central reality of the twenty-first century: the United States and Russia are no longer strategic adversaries. The Moscow Treaty on Strategic Reductions is emblematic of this new reality and reflects a critical change in Russian thinking that promises to lead to productive, long-term relations with the Euro-Atlantic community and the United States. Russia's top leaders have a realistic assessment of their country's current weakness and the policies-internal and external-needed to reverse those weaknesses. They understand, increasingly, that Cold War approaches do not serve their national interests and that Russian and American strategic interests overlap in many areas.

United States policy seeks to use this turn in Russian thinking to refocus our relationship on emerging and potential common interests and challenges. We are broadening our already extensive cooperation in the global war on terrorism. We are facilitating Russia's entry into the World Trade Organization, without lowering standards for accession, to promote beneficial bilateral trade and investment relations. We have created the NATO-Russia Council with the goal of deepening security cooperation among Russia, our European allies, and ourselves. We will continue to bolster the independence and stability of the states of the former Soviet Union in the belief that a prosperous and stable neighborhood will reinforce Russia's growing commitment to integration into the Euro-Atlantic community.

At the same time, we are realistic about the differences that still divide us from Russia and about the time and effort it will take to build an enduring strategic partnership. Lingering distrust of our motives and policies by key Russian elites slows improvement in our relations. Russia's uneven commitment to the basic values of free-market democracy and dubious record in combating the proliferation of weapons of mass destruction remain matters of great concern. Russia's very weakness limits the opportunities for cooperation. Nevertheless, those opportunities are vastly greater now than in recent years-or even decades.

The United States has undertaken a transformation in its bilateral relationship with India based on a conviction that U.S. interests require a strong relationship with India. We are the two largest democracies, committed to political freedom protected by representative government. India is moving toward greater economic freedom as well. We have a common interest in the free flow of commerce, including through the vital sea lanes of the Indian Ocean. Finally, we share an interest in fighting terrorism and in creating a strategically stable Asia.

Differences remain, including over the development of India's nuclear and missile programs, and the pace of India's economic reforms. But while in the past these concerns may have dominated our thinking about India, today we start with a view of India as a growing world power with which we have common strategic interests. Through a strong partnership with India, we can best address any differences and shape a dynamic future.

The United States relationship with China is an important part of our strategy to promote a stable, peaceful, and prosperous Asia-Pacific region. We welcome the emergence of a strong, peaceful, and prosperous China. The democratic development of China is crucial to that future. Yet, a quarter century after beginning the process of shedding the worst features of the Communist legacy, China's leaders have not yet made the next series of fundamental choices about the character of their state. In pursuing advanced military capabilities that can threaten its neighbors in the Asia-Pacific region, China is following an outdated path that, in the end, will hamper its own pursuit of national greatness. In time, China will find that social and political freedom is the only source of that greatness.

The United States seeks a constructive relationship with a changing China. We already cooperate well where our interests overlap, including the current war on terrorism and in promoting stability on the Korean peninsula. Likewise, we have coordinated on the future of Afghanistan and have initiated a comprehensive dialogue on counter-terrorism and similar transitional concerns. Shared health and environmental threats, such as the spread of HIV/AIDS, challenge us to promote jointly the welfare of our citizens.

Addressing these transnational threats will challenge China to become more open with information, promote the development of civil society, and enhance individual human rights. China has begun to take the road to political openness, permitting many personal freedoms and conducting village-level elections, yet remains strongly committed to national one-party rule by the Communist Party. To make that nation truly accountable to its citizen's needs and aspirations, however, much work remains to be done. Only by allowing the Chinese people to think, assemble, and worship freely can China reach its full potential.

Our important trade relationship will benefit from China's entry into the World Trade Organization, which will create more export opportunities and ultimately more jobs for American farmers, workers, and companies. China is our fourth largest trading partner, with over $100 billion in annual two-way trade. The power of market principles and the WTO's requirements for transparency and accountability will advance openness and the rule of law in China to help establish basic protections for commerce and for citizens. There are, however, other areas in which we have profound disagreements. Our commitment to the self-defense of Taiwan under the Taiwan Relations Act is one. Human rights is another. We expect China to adhere to its nonproliferation commitments. We will work to narrow differences where they exist, but not allow them to preclude cooperation where we agree.

The events of September 11, 2001, fundamentally changed the context for relations between the United States and other main centers of global power, and opened vast, new opportunities. With our long-standing allies in Europe and Asia, and with leaders in Russia, India, and China, we must develop active agendas of cooperation lest these relationships become routine and unproductive.

Every agency of the United States Government shares the challenge. We can build fruitful habits of consultation, quiet argument, sober analysis, and common action. In the long-term, these are the practices that will sustain the supremacy of our common principles and keep open the path of progress.

IX. Transform America's National Security Institutions to Meet the Challenges and Opportunities of the Twenty-First Century

"Terrorists attacked a symbol of American prosperity. They did not touch its source. America is successful because of the hard work, creativity, and enterprise of our people."

President Bush
Washington, D.C. (Joint Session of Congress)
September 20, 2001

The major institutions of American national security were designed in a different era to meet different requirements. All of them must be transformed. It is time to reaffirm the essential role of American military strength. We must build and maintain our defenses beyond challenge. Our military's highest priority is to defend the United States. To do so effectively, our military must:

- assure our allies and friends;
- dissuade future military competition;
- deter threats against U.S. interests, allies, and friends; and
- decisively defeat any adversary if deterrence fails.

The unparalleled strength of the United States armed forces, and their forward presence, have maintained the peace in some of the world's most strategically vital regions. However, the threats and enemies we must confront have changed, and so must our forces. A military structured to deter massive Cold War-era armies must be transformed to focus more on how an adversary might fight rather than where and when a war might occur. We will channel our energies to overcome a host of operational challenges.

The presence of American forces overseas is one of the most profound symbols of the U.S. commitments to allies and friends. Through our willingness to use force in our own defense and in defense of others, the United States demonstrates its resolve to maintain a balance of power that favors freedom. To contend with uncertainty and to meet the many security challenges we face, the United States will require bases and stations within and beyond Western Europe and Northeast Asia, as well as temporary access arrangements for the long-distance deployment of U.S. forces.

Before the war in Afghanistan, that area was low on the list of major planning contingencies. Yet, in a very short time, we had to operate across the length and breadth of that remote nation, using every branch of the armed forces. We must prepare for more such deployments by developing assets such as advanced remote sensing, long-range precision strike capabilities, and transformed maneuver and expeditionary forces. This broad portfolio of military capabilities must also include the ability to defend the homeland, conduct information operations, ensure U.S. access to distant theaters, and protect critical U.S. infrastructure and assets in outer space.

Innovation within the armed forces will rest on experimentation with new approaches to warfare, strengthening joint operations, exploiting U.S. intelligence advantages, and taking full advantage of science and technology. We must also transform the way the Department of Defense is run, especially in financial management and recruitment and retention. Finally, while maintaining near-term readiness and the ability to fight the war on terrorism, the goal must be to provide the President with a wider range of military options to discourage aggression or any form of coercion against the United States, our allies, and our friends.

We know from history that deterrence can fail; and we know from experience that some enemies cannot be deterred. The United States must and will maintain the capability to defeat any attempt by an enemy-whether a state or non-state actor-to impose its will on the United States, our allies, or our friends. We will maintain the forces sufficient to support our obligations, and to defend freedom. Our forces will be strong enough to dissuade potential adversaries from pursuing a military build-up in hopes of surpassing, or equaling, the power of the United States.

Intelligence-and how we use it-is our first line of defense against terrorists and the threat posed by hostile states. Designed around the priority of gathering enormous information about a massive, fixed object-the Soviet bloc-the intelligence community is coping with the challenge of following a far more complex and elusive set of targets.

We must transform our intelligence capabilities and build new ones to keep pace with the nature of these threats. Intelligence must be appropriately integrated with our defense and law enforcement systems and coordinated with our allies and friends. We need to protect the capabilities we have so that we do not arm our enemies with the knowledge of how best to surprise us. Those who would harm us also seek the benefit of surprise to limit our prevention and response options and to maximize injury.

We must strengthen intelligence warning and analysis to provide integrated threat assessments for national and homeland security. Since the threats inspired by foreign governments and groups may be conducted inside the United States, we must also ensure the proper fusion of information between intelligence and law enforcement.

Initiatives in this area will include:

- strengthening the authority of the Director of Central Intelligence to lead the development and actions of the Nation's foreign intelligence capabilities;
- establishing a new framework for intelligence warning that provides seamless and integrated warning across the spectrum of threats facing the nation and our allies;
- continuing to develop new methods of collecting information to sustain our intelligence advantage;
- investing in future capabilities while working to protect them through a more

vigorous effort to prevent the compromise of intelligence capabilities; and
- collecting intelligence against the terrorist danger across the government with all source analysis.

As the United States Government relies on the armed forces to defend America's interests, it must rely on diplomacy to interact with other nations. We will ensure that the Department of State receives funding sufficient to ensure the success of American diplomacy. The State Department takes the lead in managing our bilateral relationships with other governments. And in this new era, its people and institutions must be able to interact equally adroitly with non-governmental organizations and international institutions. Officials trained mainly in international politics must also extend their reach to understand complex issues of domestic governance around the world, including public health, education, law enforcement, the judiciary, and public diplomacy.

Our diplomats serve at the front line of complex negotiations, civil wars, and other humanitarian catastrophes. As humanitarian relief requirements are better understood, we must also be able to help build police forces, court systems, and legal codes, local and provincial government institutions, and electoral systems. Effective international cooperation is needed to accomplish these goals, backed by American readiness to play our part.

Just as our diplomatic institutions must adapt so that we can reach out to others, we also need a different and more comprehensive approach to public information efforts that can help people around the world learn about and understand America. The war on terrorism is not a clash of civilizations. It does, however, reveal the clash inside a civilization, a battle for the future of the Muslim world. This is a struggle of ideas and this is an area where America must excel.

We will take the actions necessary to ensure that our efforts to meet our global security commitments and protect Americans are not impaired by the potential for investigations, inquiry, or prosecution by the International Criminal Court (ICC), whose jurisdiction does not extend to Americans and which we do not accept. We will work together with other nations to avoid complications in our military operations and cooperation, through such mechanisms as multilateral and bilateral agreements that will protect U.S. nationals from the ICC. We will implement fully the American Service members Protection Act, whose provisions are intended to ensure and enhance the protection of U.S. personnel and officials.

We will make hard choices in the coming year and beyond to ensure the right level and allocation of government spending on national security. The United States Government must strengthen its defenses to win this war. At home, our most important priority is to protect the homeland for the American people.

Today, the distinction between domestic and foreign affairs is diminishing. In a globalized world, events beyond America's borders have a greater impact inside them. Our society must be open to people, ideas, and goods from across the globe. The characteristics we most cherish-our freedom, our cities, our systems of movement, and modern life-are vulnerable to terrorism. This vulnerability will persist long after we bring to justice those responsible for the

September 11 attacks. As time passes, individuals may gain access to means of destruction that until now could be wielded only by armies, fleets, and squadrons. This is a new condition of life. We will adjust to it and thrive-in spite of it.

In exercising our leadership, we will respect the values, judgment, and interests of our friends and partners. Still, we will be prepared to act apart when our interests and unique responsibilities require. When we disagree on particulars, we will explain forthrightly the grounds for our concerns and strive to forge viable alternatives. We will not allow such disagreements to obscure our determination to secure together, with our allies and our friends, our shared fundamental interests and values.

Ultimately, the foundation of American strength is at home. It is in the skills of our people, the dynamism of our economy, and the resilience of our institutions. A diverse, modern society has inherent, ambitious, entrepreneurial energy. Our strength comes from what we do with that energy. That is where our national security begins.